P9-BJG-261

Mac simply couldn't believe his eyes.

It was Ella, all right. No mistaking that. The thing he couldn't get over, get around, get past, was her…condition.

She was pregnant. With child. *Great* with child.

He watched in a daze as she moved slowly back and forth between the kitchen and the dining room. She was having a baby. Could it be his baby? Myriad emotions whipped his mind, numbing it with confusion. But his heart suffered no such bewilderment. Only longing. Oh, how he'd missed her. How he yearned for her still. After everything.

She had hurt him deeply, and now…now he'd discovered that she was about to have a child.

His child…

Dear Reader,

July brings you the fifth title of Silhouette Romance's VIRGIN BRIDES promotion. This series is devoted to the beautiful metaphor of the traditional white wedding and the fairy-tale magic of innocence awakened to passionate love on the wedding night. In perennial favorite Sandra Steffen's offering, *The Bounty Hunter's Bride,* a rugged loner finds himself propositioned by the innocent beauty who'd nursed him to health in a remote mountain cabin. He resists her precious gift…but winds up her shotgun groom when her father and four brothers discover their hideaway!

Diana Whitney returns to the Romance lineup with *One Man's Promise,* a wonderfully warmhearted story about a struggling FABULOUS FATHER and an adventurous single gal who are brought together by their love for his little girl and a shaggy mutt named Rags. And THE BRUBAKER BRIDES are back! In *Cinderella's Secret Baby,* the third book of Carolyn Zane's charming series, tycoon Mac Brubaker tracks down the poor but proud bride who'd left him the day after their whirlwind wedding, only to discover she's about to give birth to the newest Brubaker heir.…

Wanted: A Family Forever is confirmed bachelor Zach Robinson's secret wish in this intensely emotional story by Anne Peters. But will marriage-jaded Monica Griffith and her little girl trust him with their hearts? Linda Varner's twentieth book for Silhouette is book two of THREE WEDDINGS AND A FAMILY. When two go-getters learn they must marry to achieve their dreams, a wedding of convenience results in a *Make-Believe Husband*…and many sleepless nights! Finally, a loyal assistant agrees to be her boss's *Nine-to-Five Bride* in Robin Wells's sparkling new story, but of course this wife wants her new husband to be a *permanent* acquisition!

Enjoy each and every Silhouette Romance!

Regards,

Joan Marlow Golan

Joan Marlow Golan
Senior Editor Silhouette Books

Please address questions and book requests to:
Silhouette Reader Service
U.S.: 3010 Walden Ave., P.O. Box 1325, Buffalo, NY 14269
Canadian: P.O. Box 609, Fort Erie, Ont. L2A 5X3

CINDERELLA'S SECRET BABY

Carolyn Zane

Silhouette
ROMANCE™
Published by Silhouette Books
America's Publisher of Contemporary Romance

If you purchased this book without a cover you should be aware
that this book is stolen property. It was reported as "unsold and
destroyed" to the publisher, and neither the author nor the
publisher has received any payment for this "stripped book."

For all my female cousins: Grace, Brenda, Elaine,
Wendy, Joanne, Ronda, Holly and…Karen, Joanie and
Laura, wherever you are. I have been blessed with the
sweetest group of women cousins. You are all dolls, and
though you occasionally find your names among my
pages, the adjectives that actually apply are kind,
talented, witty, sexy, voluptuous and beautiful!

THANK YOU, Dear Lord.

 SILHOUETTE BOOKS

ISBN 0-373-19308-4

CINDERELLA'S SECRET BABY

Copyright © 1998 by Carolyn Suzanne Pizzuti

All rights reserved. Except for use in any review, the reproduction
or utilization of this work in whole or in part in any form by any
electronic, mechanical or other means, now known or hereafter
invented, including xerography, photocopying and recording, or in
any information storage or retrieval system, is forbidden without
the written permission of the editorial office, Silhouette Books,
300 East 42nd Street, New York, NY 10017 U.S.A.

All characters in this book have no existence outside the imagination of
the author and have no relation whatsoever to anyone bearing the same
name or names. They are not even distantly inspired by any individual
known or unknown to the author, and all incidents are pure invention.

This edition published by arrangement with Harlequin Books S.A.

® and TM are trademarks of Harlequin Books S.A., used under license.
Trademarks indicated with ® are registered in the United States Patent
and Trademark Office, the Canadian Trade Marks Office and in other
countries.

Printed in U.S.A.

CAROLYN ZANE

lives with her husband, Matt, and her toddler daughter, Madeline, in the scenic rolling countryside near Portland, Oregon's Willamette River. Like Chevy Chase's character in the movie *Funny Farm,* Carolyn finally decided to trade in a decade of city dwelling and producing local television commercials for the quaint country life of a novelist. And, even though they have bitten off decidedly more than they can chew in the remodeling of their hundred-plus-year-old farmhouse, life is somewhat saner for her than for poor Chevy. The neighbors are friendly, the mail carrier actually stops at the box and the dog, Bob Barker, sticks close to home.

THE BRUBAKER FAMILY
of Texas

Big Daddy - m. - Miss Clarise

| Conway (a.k.a. Bru) | Merle (a.k.a. Mac) | Buck | Patsy | Johnny | Kenny | Waylon | Willie | Hank |

Conway (a.k.a. Bru)
m.
Penelope Wainright

Merle (a.k.a. Mac)
m.
Ella McCloskey

Buck
m.
Holly Fergusson

Waylon — Willie (twins)

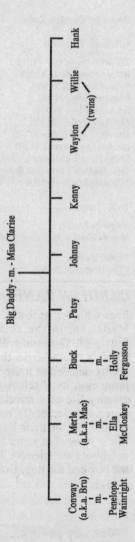

Chapter One

"Stop! Don't eat that!"

"Why not?" Mac Brubaker looked at the meatball dripping with sauce that he held between his fingertips and frowned. He was starving and this looked delicious. So what if it was for some social shindig his folks had planned for that evening? He shrugged. Nobody would miss one lousy meatball. He popped it into his mouth. Interesting flavor.

"Because," the sultry voice that came from over his shoulder continued sweetly, "it's dog food."

"*Gog* foog?" he mumbled. Frozen, his face mirrored the revulsion that suddenly filled his belly. His lips curled back over his teeth as he wondered what to do next.

"Yes. Straight out of the can," said the helpful feminine voice. "SuperDog dog chow. Fortified with vitamins, iron and eighty percent actual meat by-product," she parroted as she read aloud from the label. "For the—" a bubble of mirth squeaked past her lips "—superdog in your life."

"Mea...by-pawuck?" Mac mumbled without looking

behind him to discover the source of this informative and humor leaden voice. Striding rapidly to the sink, he spat out the contents of his mouth. Then, gasping for air, he inhaled some SuperDog dog chow down the wrong pipe and was suddenly sent into a most undignified coughing fit.

Bertha, the Brubaker family's grumpy weekend kitchen supervisor, placed her fists on her well-padded hips and scowled across the enormous room, first at the coughing Mac, and then at the young woman who stood behind him, bent over with laughter.

"Mac Brubaker, what are you doin' here in my kitchen, tryin' to choke yourself to death?" Bertha shouted churlishly. Her wiry red and gray hair, like the wispy feathers of an ostrich plume, stood out at absurd angles on the sides of her head.

"He accidentally ate some of Chubby's dog food," the feminine voice laughingly informed Bertha.

"Ah hammmm, ah hachh," Mac sputtered.

"Ella." Bertha gesticulated wildly, setting her arms into motion. "Stop laughin' and get this boy a cup of water, before he kills himself," the cranky woman snapped.

"Yes, ma'am," the young woman Bertha had referred to as Ella responded.

Much to Mac's consternation, Ella was laughing like a punch-drunk hyena now. Running to the water cooler, she quickly filled a cup with water then, rushing back, pressed it into his hands. "There you go," she giggled.

"Ella, get back to work," Bertha ordered. "The show's over."

Sobering slightly, Ella shot a sideways glance at Bertha, then smiled at Mac. "Yes, ma'am," she answered agreeably before doing as she was bid.

"Thank you," Mac croaked to Ella, blinking back the tears that blurred his vision, and downed the cool, refreshing water. She was truly an angel. He listened in annoyance as muffled peals of hilarity still issued forth from somewhere behind him. Okay, she was truly an annoying angel. Whoever she was. He hadn't gotten a good look at her yet.

Slowly he brought himself upright and glanced over his shoulder. Like two planets colliding, his gaze slammed into hers with a violent force that caused the wind to whoosh from his lungs.

Abruptly she stopped laughing and stared at him.

Mac's heart hammered so fiercely, he was sure Bertha might try to wrestle him to the ground and attempt to administer CPR.

Lord, have mercy.

His jaw dropped and his pupils dilated.

Orchestral strains of "Some Enchanted Evening" suddenly swelled in his brain. Was he seeing things? Good heavens above, who was this celestial vision? She had to be brand-new to the Brubaker kitchen because he would definitely know if he'd seen her before.

Twilight streamed through the large French doors at the end of the enormous Brubaker kitchen, casting an ethereal glow over the room and bathing the beautiful Ella in its magic. Stainless-steel appliances, copper pots and pans, mahogany cabinets and marble countertops gave the room a rich warmth in the cool, early evening. Autumn breezes gently billowed white gauzy curtains that draped the windows and puddled richly on the floor.

Dazed, Mac watched as Ella blinked, took a deep breath and shook her head as if to clear it. Slowly her gaze traveled from his, to the bowl of dog food, and her lips twitched. Moving over to the counter, she collected the empty dog food can and tossed it into the recycling bin, then set the bowl on the back stoop for the lazy Chubby.

All the while she battled back the broad grin that was tugging at her mouth.

Thunderation, Mac thought fuzzily, she was beautiful. His eyes roved over her long, shapely legs, then up to her gamine face with those snapping blue eyes and full kissable lips. Thick waves of her fluffy blond hair were swept into a loose braid that trailed down the middle of her back. It was a simple, unsophisticated style, but on her, it was somehow regal. Even the frumpish uniform she wore took on a certain class as it clung to her athletic curves.

Ever alert, Bertha noticed his thorough scrutiny of her new pastry chef. "You met Ella yet?"

"Uh." Mac cleared his throat. "No."

"Ella," Bertha shouted and waved the young woman back to her side. "Come here, child." Wiping her hands on her apron, Ella joined them. "This here's Mac Brubaker, Big Daddy Brubaker's second son. He helps his older brother Bru run their father's business down there at Brubaker International," Bertha told Ella and jabbed a finger into Mac's chest.

"Oh. So you're one of the bosses. I'm, uh, you know, sorry I laughed," Ella said contritely. The twinkle in her eye said otherwise.

Puckering her spongy face into a thoughtful bunch, Bertha looked up at Mac. "What is it you do again, boy?"

"CEO, oil refinery division," Mac heard himself respond breathily. Sheez. He sounded like a dork. A love-struck dork.

"That sounds interesting." Ella made an attempt at polite conversation.

"Not really."

"Oh." Ella shrugged.

Mac winced. Yep. Make that a love-struck super dork.

"I helped raise him from a pup," Bertha loudly informed Ella, much to Mac's eternal chagrin.

For some absurd reason, he didn't want Ella thinking of him as a…pup. Especially considering the thoughts that were flitting through his mind were anything but puppy love.

"And, Mac," Bertha continued, "this here's Ella McCloskey, our new pastry chef. Today's her first day." To Ella she queried, "That is your last name? McCloskey, right?"

Ella nodded.

"Your kin live around these parts?" Bertha wondered.

A wary look flashed briefly into the young woman's eyes. Squaring her shoulders, Ella shook her head. "No. I don't have any family to speak of," she stated matter-of-factly.

"None?" Mac choked, his throat still ticklish. He was surprised. He couldn't imagine life without an army of relatives under his feet.

Ella hesitated as if deciding how much to reveal to this virtual stranger. "Not really," she shrugged. "Just me, and a few steprelatives I haven't seen for a long time."

Mac's heart picked up speed. *She was single.* How fortunate for him, being that he was in the process of falling in love with her.

This woman fascinated him in his first moments of observing her, as no woman he'd ever met before. Something about her was completely different than the rest of the young women in his social circle.

It wasn't the clothes she wore, for the uniform had as much style as a potato sack. And it wasn't the trendy hairstyle, as stray wisps of hair escaped her braid and gave her a rather windswept look. No, it wasn't anything so obvious as fancy perfume or makeup, nor was it a large vocabulary that spoke of years of education. Because, though her voice was low and cultured, she spoke simply and answered the curmudgeonly Bertha with a wonderful sense of humor and seemingly limitless patience.

He could tell just by the way she carried herself that she was proud but not vain, gentle yet filled with inner strength, and sweet, but full of spunk, too.

He dragged a hand across his face. Good grief, he was waxing poetic. How could he possibly know all of this about her after only a few minutes in her presence?

He couldn't.

But he had a gut feeling about her. Something deep down inside told him that she could be the one. His heart constricted with some nameless emotion as he stood watching her, his throat went dry all over again and he had to clear it before he choked.

"Ah hemm, ah hachh," he wheezed.

"You gonna be okay, boy?" Bertha demanded, taking the water cup he still held in his hands and tossing it into the sink. Quite obviously, she still thought of him as the one who—diapers drooping—would beg Popsicles from her in the hot summer months so many years ago. She pounded him between the shoulder blades a few times for good measure.

"When you stop beating me, I'll surely improve," Mac joshed, patting the red-faced woman on her time-weathered cheeks.

"Good," she barked as if she couldn't have cared less, "because I have to check on the goodies I'm fixin' for your daddy's social tonight. What are you doin' here, anyway?"

Casting a sheepish glance at Ella, he said, "I worked late today and missed lunch. And, I don't really have the energy for whatever social occasion is going on in the dining room tonight."

Bertha snorted. "Ella, fix this big lug something to eat, then take a dinner break yourself. When you come back, I want you to give me a hand with the hors d'oeuvres for Big Daddy's little get-together."

With that curt directive, the older woman shuffled across the room and thrusting her generous fanny topside, yanked open the oven door. Her head disappeared into the appliance's cavernous belly, as she commenced poking the prime rib she was preparing for the buffet table.

"You don't have to fix my dinner," Mac murmured to Ella, keeping his voice low so that Bertha would have no reason to complain. The kitchen was Bertha's domain during the weekends, and like a good drill sergeant, she didn't tolerate any folderol.

"I don't mind," Ella protested. "It's part of my job."

Bringing her gaze to his she regarded him so guilelessly, that he felt his throat begin to close again. What was happening to him? he wondered, taken aback by his reaction to Ella. Her eyes probed his with a blatant curiosity, and Mac wondered if she was feeling the same restlessness swirl in the pit of his stomach that he was. As their gazes held and locked, Mac froze. No. She couldn't be feeling what he was and still look so collected.

She was probably simply thinking that he was a dork.

"So. This is your first day," he finally was able to croak. Nothing like stating the obvious, he silently berated himself.

"Yes." She tucked a stray tendril of hair behind her ear. "It's my first day."

Mentally Mac made a note of the autumn date in his mind. After all, it wasn't every day that he fell head over heels in love. And he was falling in love, of that he was more certain than even his name. Had anyone tried to convince him of the validity of love at first sight before he'd walked into the kitchen that day, he'd have laughed them out of the room. But after a few glorious moments in her presence, he was a believer.

Pulling up a bar stool, Mac sat down and studied Ella's pretty face from across the island countertop. He wanted to know more about this pink-cheeked doll with the mischievous spark in her large blue eyes.

"What would you like to eat?" Ella asked, bracing her arms against the island and leaning toward him.

"Oh, anything would be fine."

Ella *tsked* playfully. "Well, certainly we can do better than SuperDog dog chow."

He rolled his eyes as her face scrunched with amusement. She gestured to the refrigerator. "It's only my first day on the job, but I'm sure I can scare up a sandwich and a bowl of soup, if you're interested."

"I'm interested." Mac blinked his glassy-eyed stare away. "Uh, you know, uh, in the sandwich. Soup sounds great, too."

"Tomato soup?"

"Wonderful." His eyes scrutinized the heart shape of her face.

"How about a grilled cheese sandwich?"

"Perfect," he breathed, as his gaze dropped to her lips.

Nodding, Ella moved to the cabinets and began searching for ingredients.

"So. Who's Big Daddy throwing this little get-together for tonight?" Mac asked, attempting to sound casual.

"From what I gather, some old neighbors and friends of the family are coming to visit from Oklahoma. Some folks named—" she frowned thoughtfully as she tugged a loaf of bread out of the bread box "—Ferguson?"

"The Fergusons?" Mac's face fell.

"Uh-huh. Anyway, your dad is throwing a little reunion

for them with some of their old friends." Ella paused and looked up at him. "What's wrong? Don't you like the Fergusons?"

"No, no, it's not that." He couldn't very well explain to Ella that once Big Daddy corralled him into one of these social gatherings, he would be expected to make pleasant chitchat for hours with people he barely remembered. Or at least until he feared his head would cave in.

Lacing his fingers he cradled his chin and watched her open a can of soup, scoop it into a microwave bowl and add some water. "So, Ella." He cleared his throat, eyed her in what he hoped was a nonchalant manner and tactfully changed the subject. "Where are you from?"

"Originally?" A smile played on her lips as she glanced at him, then went back to whisking the lumps out of the soup.

"Sure." Angling his head, he watched and waited for her response.

Ella hesitated. This was her first day on the job. How much of her wacky past did she want to reveal to her brand-new employer? Well, technically *he* wasn't her employer, his father was. But still, she really needed this job, and desperately wished to put her best foot forward. Although, she thought ruefully, laughing at his dog food snack certainly hadn't furthered that particular quest. A grin stole across her face.

It's just that he was so darn cute. And, that made her nervous. Really nervous. She didn't want to find him nearly as attractive as she did. It wasn't good for her long-term career plans.

Mac Brubaker was just like a prince out of a fairy tale. Thick, golden brown hair. Pearly white teeth. Deep and mischievous dimples. Velvety brown eyes. Not to mention his long, lanky legs, narrow hips and broad shoulders.

And the way he looked at her? It was enough to set off spontaneous combustion.

She fumbled with the whisk.

"England," she finally volunteered and tried to think of a graceful way to change the subject.

"You don't sound British."

Ella laughed. "That's because I was only there for a few months. Where are you from?"

"Here." He lifted and dropped a shoulder as if that answered that. "Then where did you go?"

Glancing into his deep brown eyes, Ella sighed. Already she suspected that Mac Brubaker would worm far more information out of her than she was usually wont to discuss. Especially with a stranger. It was those eyes. Those heavily fringed, velvety, chocolaty eyes that mesmerized her into a supreme feeling of trust and confidence in a man she barely knew.

"Well, my mother passed away when I was just a baby. Complications from childbirth." Ella gave her head a slight shake. "According to my father, she never regained her strength after I was born."

"I'm sorry," Mac murmured.

"Me, too." Her smile was wistful. "Anyway, heartbroken, my father returned with me to Southern California."

"So it's just the two of you?"

"No. Just before I entered my teens, my father decided I needed a mother and some siblings. So, he married my stepmother and adopted her two daughters."

Mac grinned. "Was she an evil stepmother?"

Ella froze. He was teasing. Unfortunately he really didn't know how close to home he was hitting.

A solemn expression of contrition crossed his face. "I'm sorry. I didn't mean to pry."

"No, no. I know. It's just that..." She paused. He would

make a wonderful interviewer. Suddenly she wanted him to know every ridiculous detail of her rather dysfunctional family life. It must be the light of understanding in his expression. Or, perhaps it was the twin dimples that spoke of a lifetime of good humor. She took a deep breath. He seemed genuinely interested. What the heck, she decided and with a shrug, gamely plunged in. She so rarely had anyone show this kind of interest. Perhaps it would be good for her.

"Maybe you've heard of my stepmother? Stormy Winters? For years she played Delilah Chastaine on the soap 'Secret Lives.'"

"Delilah Chastaine?" Angling his head, Mac regarded her as she programmed the microwave. "Isn't she the psychopath who ran over her ex-husband's first wife with her Ferrari, or something like that?"

Openmouthed, Ella stared at him. "Very good! Do you watch 'Secret Lives'?"

"No. Bertha did, back when she worked weekdays." He pointed at the television that sat on the countertop, in the corner.

"Oh, no." Ella stuck out her tongue in distaste.

"So, what was life like, with Stormy Winters?"

"Well," Ella said over her shoulder as she dug the griddle out of the appliance cupboard, "let's just say that she and Delilah Chastaine have a lot in common."

"Really? She doesn't own a Ferrari, does she?"

"No," she responded with a grin. "And it's a good thing or I probably wouldn't be standing here talking to you."

Mac grimaced in sympathy. "That bad, huh?"

"Yep." She wouldn't go into detail about Stormy's myriad abuses. That was all in her past. Despite her stepmother's gloomy prophecy to the contrary, Ella knew that she would succeed in this life on her own. No one would ever tell her otherwise again.

"You said she had two daughters?"

"Mmm-hmm." Ella hummed as she oiled the griddle and assembled the cheese sandwiches. "Phoenix and Arizona."

"Phoenix and Arizona?" His jaw dropped. "Man, and I thought Big Daddy gave us strange names."

"Stormy had a flair for the dramatic in everything she did. Besides, Mac isn't a strange name."

Mac grinned ruefully up at her. "Merle. After Merle Haggard."

Ella's lips curved.

"He named all nine of us kids after his favorite country singers." Holding up his fingers Mac ticked them off for her edification. "Conway is my older brother, and goes by the nickname Bru. He was named for Conway Twitty."

"Oh my."

"Yeah. He had more than his share of fistfights in school over it. But I think it made him tough." Mac dimpled. "Then, after me, there are Buck, Patsy, Johnny, Kenny, the twins Waylon and Willie and last but not least, little Hank."

"Wow. That's a big family."

"Yep. So are Phoenix and Alabama your only sisters?"

"Arizona," Ella responded and laughed. "Yes. After my father passed away it was just the four of us."

An amused quirk tugged at his mouth. "That's classic. The evil stepmother and the two ugly stepsisters."

"I know it sounds cliché, but as a family unit, we were anything but typical." Still smiling, Ella dropped his sandwiches on the now-sizzling griddle. "And I never said they were ugly."

"They couldn't have been half as pretty as you are."

Ella rolled her eyes. "They were lovely. They were just spoiled. And after so many years of being coddled, they went into a bit of a culture shock when Stormy lost all her money. Then she lost our inheritance from my father."

"How'd she do that?"

Exhaling heavily, Ella glanced up at him. "Remember when Delilah Chastaine swallowed that liquid pipe cleaner that Raven and Damion poured into her cocktail, she went into a coma and never recovered?"

Mac shrugged. "No, but Bertha would be able to act it out and quote the lines verbatim."

"Now *that*, I'd like to see." Ella laughed as she cooked his grilled cheese sandwiches. When they were done, she loaded a plate and passed it to him. Then, moving to the microwave, she retrieved his soup and set it next to his plate.

"Anyway, after her character went into the coma, Stormy's contract was up with 'Secret Lives,' and the big guns at the network decided not to renew. For a long time, I think Stormy hoped that they would bring her back as Delilah's evil psychopathic twin." Ella paused and arched a sardonic brow. "If you can imagine anyone more evil or psychopathic than Delilah. But, her contract was never renewed, and Stormy was out of a job. That was extremely hard for her to accept. There were some pretty—" pausing she grimaced "—*lean* times when I was a teenager. And," she mused, her eyes glazed with the memories, "I suppose having me around didn't help matters. I think she resented having the extra mouth to feed."

"That's too bad."

"Well, it's all in the past now." Ella cast off the haunted look that had filled her eyes. "To make it up to her, I did all the cooking, and cleaning," she said brightly, "which, as it turns out, was a good education. When I was eighteen

I moved to Texas to strike out on my own. That was eight years ago. I've been cooking here and there ever since.''

"Mmm-hmm." Mac's appreciative groan told her he was well pleased with his meal.

As he ate, the conversation took many turns until, before either of them could believe it, he'd finished both his sandwiches, polished off a bowl of soup, two bananas and a pile of Ella's chocolate chip cookies.

"Oh…" he groaned. "I ate too much."

"Good," Ella said with an indulgent smile.

"So, do you like it here so far?" he inquired, hoping that she was going to be around for a while. Fifty, sixty years would have suited him just fine, he thought foggily. He stared at the place where the high apple of her cheek gave way to the hollow above her jaw. Such a kissable spot.

Her gaze shot to his. "So far I…like it."

Mac smiled, gratified. He gestured toward Bertha whose face was flushed beet red from exertion as she bustled around at the far end of the kitchen. "Bertha says you can take a dinner break if you want to."

Glancing over her shoulder, Ella nodded. "Yes, she did, but I'm not really hungry yet."

Mac pushed back his chair and crumpling his napkin, tossed it on his plate. "You don't have to be hungry to need a break," he teased. His voice loaded with meaning, he lifted a brow at the grunting Bertha.

Ella's lilting laughter filled the air, and it was then that Mac's fate was sealed. "I guess not," she agreed with a good-natured shrug.

"Come on then," he urged and offered her his hand, "and I'll give you the nickel tour. After all, it is your first day on the job. Somebody has to show you around." He shrugged in what he hoped was an artless, confident manner. Inside, his stomach was a churning sea of vulnerability. It was idiotic how much he wanted her to walk the grounds with him.

"I'd like that," she murmured, tentatively reaching out and taking his proffered hand. "I'd like that a lot."

"The Fergusons ought to be here in an hour," Big Daddy Brubaker chortled as he joined his wife, Miss Clarise, out on the lower veranda of their elegant Southern mansion. The diminutive patriarch of the large Brubaker family settled into the porch swing next to her and reaching between them, took her hand in his.

Lines forked at the corners of Miss Clarise's deep blue eyes as she regarded her husband of over thirty years.

"I'm surely looking forward to seeing George and Trudy again," Miss Clarise murmured in her soft drawl. Slowly they swung back and forth, enjoying the panoramic sunset on the Texas horizon. The autumn sky was especially lovely tonight. "It's too bad that Holly couldn't join us this evening. Why, I don't believe we've seen her since she was six or seven, and playing with Mac and Buck."

Nearly twenty years ago, the Fergusons had been the Brubakers' closest neighbors and friends. Then, George had struck oil on his Oklahoma spread, and moved his family north to tend his fields there.

"The times I've spoken with George on the phone, he tells me that she's wilder than a March hare." Big Daddy's rubbery face split into a nostalgic grin. "Old George is fit to be tied. Claims she's only interested in working down at the Miracle House children's shelter, and dodging his best efforts to get her settled down and married."

Over the years, the adults had vacationed together from time to time, and kept the close relationship alive. But none of their offspring had accompanied them on these little jaunts, so they hadn't seen each others' children since they were just tykes.

Miss Clarise frowned thoughtfully as she tucked a graying tendril back into her tidy chignon. "I think it's admirable that Holly wants to help underprivileged children. Frankly, Big Daddy, I'm somewhat surprised at George's attitude."

"Oh, I think George doesn't object to her working down at the shelter as much as he would like to see her settle down and get married. Give him some grandchildren. She's twenty-seven now."

"Land sakes, Big Daddy, that's hardly old. Why, Mac will be twenty-nine soon, and he's still not married," she said pointedly, referring to their second son.

"I know!" he sputtered. "And that's exactly why I'm with George. It's high time these kids started thinking about the future. It's indecent the way they all ignore our inspirin' advice and run around like a bunch of spoiled brats, thinkin' they have forever to figure out what they want to do with their lives." Brooding, Big Daddy squinted off into the sunset.

With a heavy sigh, Miss Clarise regarded her husband's time-weathered face. She could fairly see the wheels turning in his head.

Now that Big Daddy's three oldest boys were all reaching the ripe old age of thirty, he'd made it his primary goal in life to get his rowdy sons all polished up, hitched to nice girls and working on a passel of grandbabies for him to spoil. So far, Big Daddy had been lucky. Without even trying, he'd managed to get his oldest son, Bru, married off to the plucky little image consultant Penelope Wainright that he'd hired over the summer to clean up his sons' images and get them ready for business and marriage. He hadn't expected to strike pay dirt quite so quickly, but no one could have been more pleased. Last month's fantastic September wedding had been the talk of Texas for weeks.

To Big Daddy Brubaker, nothing was more sacred than family. It was very important to him that each of his offspring find the love and happiness that he'd found with Miss Clarise. Everything else in Big Daddy's life paled in comparison to the importance of his family, including his billion-dollar bank account, his rambling antebellum mansion known as the Circle B.O.—for Brubaker Oil—his thousands of acres of Texas ranch land, his half-dozen Fortune 500 companies, or his many productive oil fields.

"Big Daddy," Miss Clarise said warily, as she studied the sudden grin of delight that crept over his pliable face, "just what, in heaven's name, have you got up your sleeve now?" Pointing her toe, she touched the porch floor and slowed the gentle sway of the swing.

"Well now, honey pie, just about the finest idea I've ever had."

"Big Daddy..." With a sigh, Miss Clarise closed her eyes and slumped against the back of the swing. "What idea?"

"I don't know why I didn't think of it ages ago!" Excited, he wildly jostled the swing as he wriggled around to face her. "We need to talk to George tonight about having him send Holly down for a visit next summer."

Opening one eye, Miss Clarise lolled her head to the side and shot a dubious look at her enthusiastic husband. "Why?"

"Don't you see?" he crowed. "For Mac!"

"For Mac?"

"Of course! Holly needs a husband. Mac needs a wife. It's perfect. Can't you just feature it? Why, I have a feelin' that those two were made for each other!"

"Big Daddy," Miss Clarise gently reminded him, "they haven't seen each other in nearly twenty years."

"So? They got along fine as kids, didn't they? Why by the end of the summer, our family and the fine Ferguson family will be united in wedded bliss. In-laws. Mutual grandbabies." His eyes rolled back in his head with the rapture of it all. "Oh, it's almost too good to be true." Sniffing, he blinked and struggled valiantly to pull himself together.

"Big Daddy, don't you think you're jumping the gun?"

"Lamb doodle," Big Daddy sighed, his furry brows forming a wiry line above his eyes as he trained his gaze back out toward the sunset. "I'm givin' George all winter to convince his little girl to come on down for a spell. That's plenty of time. Besides, I'm afraid the gun has gone and jumped us," he mused, refocusing on his second son Mac as he sauntered through the rose garden. "In fact, why wait till summer? Let's have Holly come in the spring."

"Why the rush?" Miss Clarise asked.

"See for yourself."

Tucking her chin into her shoulder and twisting in her seat, Miss Clarise followed her husband's gaze. "Isn't that the new kitchen girl with Mac?"

"Uh-huh."

"What's her name...Ella McCloskey?"

"Yep."

Hired for her ability to bake the most tantalizing pastries Big Daddy had ever tasted, her sweet nature and lovely countenance had already won the older man's undying affection. Big Daddy frowned at the familiar way Mac was teasing Ella. The young woman's lilting laughter floated on the light spring breezes as she and Mac strolled through the evening twilight.

"Yep," Big Daddy huffed with a shake of his head.

"We need to get him settled down before he chases some of the finest members of our staff off with his flirtatious ways."

"Looks to me," Miss Clarise murmured, "as if you might just be too late."

Chapter Two

Chapter Two

Two months later to the day, Ella was standing in the kitchen, her heart crowding into her throat as she set her rolling pin on the counter.

Mac was here.

She could feel it.

A smile, beginning at the corners of her mouth, spread across her entire body and a glorious, giddy feeling of excitement swelled beneath her breast. Turning, she discovered him. She had only been working in the Brubaker kitchen for two months now, but already she could sense his presence without looking.

Slowly she lifted her eyes to him, valiantly attempting to maintain an outward appearance of calm, even as a tropical storm swept through her mind. He stood leaning against the door frame that led to the rose garden while he watched her work, his arms folded across his powerful chest. The dimples that bracketed his finely sculpted lips were tugged out of hiding by his sexy smile. He was magnificent, she thought, suddenly feeling dizzy. Trembling with excitement, she brought her fluttering hands to her apron and smoothed it down over her crisply starched uniform.

They were alone in the opulent, sunny Brubaker kitchen, except for the curmudgeonly Bertha whose disapproving stare was nearly palpable in its intensity.

Pushing off the door's casing, Mac casually stepped into the enormous, fragrant room and sauntered over to stand behind Ella. Tingles of delight skittered down her spine as he placed his hand lightly on her hip and leaning against her side, whispered in her ear.

"Meet me in fifteen minutes, behind the rose garden fountain," he murmured, giving her an affectionate squeeze. "I'll walk you through the maze." His breath was warm on her neck, his voice low.

She touched her tongue to dampen her lips as she peeked over at Bertha's stony expression.

The older woman viciously hacked a head of cabbage in two with a cleaver. Lips pursed into a tight bunch, her censure shimmered across the immense chopping block.

Ella ducked her head into Mac's shoulder and whispered, "Make it twenty. I get my lunch break in twenty minutes."

Bertha shot them a stern look as she swept a pile of chopped cabbage into a large, stainless-steel bowl.

"I'll be waiting," he growled in that lazy, corporate cowboy way of his. "Behind the fountain," he reminded her, with a tug on the braid that lay against her back.

He was so wonderful, Ella thought, gazing after him. Everything about him screamed male, and her first impression of him—when their eyes had slammed together the morning they'd met—had been that of raw passion. Mac Brubaker exuded an animal magnetism, a blatant virility that no woman under the age of ninety could miss.

Oh, she sighed, watching him dazedly, he could easily

walk onto the set of any movie and star as the hero. She watched in amusement as he ambled over to Bertha, snagged a piece of the carrot she was now so madly chopping and popped it into his mouth with a charming grin. Tossing an affectionate arm around the feisty woman's plump shoulders, he kissed her ruddy cheek, and she smiled in spite of herself.

He shot Ella one last meaningful look before he strolled out the door and disappeared into the spring sunshine.

Ella felt as if she just might burst from the wonderful, euphoric feelings that were expanding in her chest. Her heart slamming wildly against her ribs, she turned back to her chores without a word to Bertha who was still eyeing her narrowly over the chopping block.

She didn't owe Bertha an explanation, she thought defiantly, deciding it best to ignore her supervisor's steely expression. After all, she hadn't done anything wrong. Why, for heaven's sake, she deserved a lunch break as much as anyone else on the kitchen staff.

"You shouldn't be gettin' too friendly with them Brubaker boys." Bertha finally gave voice to her opinion. "That's a good way to get yourself fired." It was a thinly veiled threat.

Ella's pulse throbbed high in her throat. She couldn't bear the idea of getting fired and having to leave in disgrace. To Ella, working in the Brubaker kitchen was a dream come true. This was the stepping-stone she needed to reach her goal. All her life she'd dreamed of attending a culinary institute and becoming a chef. Perhaps someday she might even own a bakery, or a restaurant.

The pitiful hand-to-mouth existence she'd led living with the eccentric Stormy and her two clueless daughters was over. Ella was on her own. And she would make it. She was nobody's whipping boy anymore, she thought defiantly. Not even Bertha's.

Ella was proud and hardworking.

That's what had drawn Big Daddy to her when she was a baker down at the Jubilee Rib-O-Rama. He'd taken one bite of her peach cobbler and hired her on the spot. Since that time, Ella had teased him about being her fairy godfather, which tickled Big Daddy to no end. He liked her wit, he loved her cooking but most of all, he just plain adored *her*.

And, the feeling was mutual. Ella couldn't let him down by ending up in some kind of trouble with her supervisor after such a short time on the job. Sighing heavily, she valiantly tried to tune Bertha out as the older woman continued to dress her down.

"So, watch out, girl," came the older woman's ominous directive, "or you'll find yourself out of here so fast your head will spin."

Lifting her chin, Ella leveled her unwavering gaze on Bertha. "I don't know what you're talking about."

"Oh," Bertha said smugly. "I think you do. Look at you, girl." She raised the cleaver and gestured loosely at the stains on Ella's apron. "You ain't got no call to go fraternizing with them rich folks. That Mac, he's just stringing you along. He don't love you. He's just toyin' with you. And why not?" she sighed and leaned heavily against the chopping block, her tired gaze scanning Ella's youthful frame. "You're easy on his eyes with that smooth complexion and trim waist. But let me tell you something. A full head of beautiful, long, blond hair ain't what that boy needs."

"Is that so?" Ella asked, feigning a confidence she only wished she was feeling. Reaching behind her neck, she pulled the thick braid that lay against her back over her shoulder and nervously twisted it in her fingers. "And how would you know what he needs?"

"Because I know this family," Bertha snapped. "I've been here since before you were knee high to a toadstool, little girl, and I aim to keep this job till you're nothing but a memory around here." Slowly the older woman shook her head and regarded her young assistant. "I happen to know for sure that Big Daddy Brubaker is working on getting all of his boys married to the daughters of rich men and important folks."

"Is that so?" A small puff of air escaped Ella's slack lips. She could scarcely believe what was coming out of this woman's mouth. Did Bertha really think that Mac Brubaker would allow his father to pick out his wife? She may be the new kid around the Brubaker chopping block, but if there was one thing she knew for sure: Mac was most definitely his own man.

Still, Bertha's scathing diatribe was beginning to get under her skin. It was true. She was not from Mac's social circle. But that shouldn't stop them from falling in love. Should it? Nervously she plucked at the rubber band that fastened her braid and cast her gaze to the floor as Bertha continued.

"Yes. That *is* so. And you'd better learn to accept the facts, Ella. That's just the way it is in these circles. You could never fit in. Never. Not unless you got a rich papa stashed away somewhere. You'd better guard your heart, girl, cause you're setting yourself up for a world of hurt."

Flames of mortification licked Ella's cheeks. Taking a deep breath, she willed her pulse to slow. Deep in her soul, she secretly feared that Bertha's words were true. But if that were so, if she and Mac really were worlds apart, why did he make her feel as if she were the richest woman in the world with one simple kiss? It couldn't be true, she thought defiantly. The world had changed. Arranged marriage was an archaic practice. These days, no matter what the person's station in life, love could conquer all. Couldn't it? She worried the inside of her cheek between her teeth.

Tossing her head, she hoped to appear as if she didn't care what the stodgy old Bertha thought. "What I do on my lunch break is my business, Bertha, and I'll thank you to mind yours."

"Don't say I didn't warn ya," the older woman sang as she went back to attacking her vegetables. "And as far as your lunch break goes, just don't dally today. I want to watch my stories."

Rattled, Ella picked up her rolling pin and slowly began to roll out the pie crust she'd been preparing for the Brubakers' evening dessert. As she worked, Bertha's words echoed in her mind.

Just what did she think she was doing? Was it really so wrong to get mixed up with Mac? As poor as a country church mouse, she had nothing to offer him. Not unless he counted her talents in the kitchen. Was she crazy to think that she could ever be considered by anyone such as Mac as marriage material?

Yes, she thought, sighing to herself. She was crazy. Crazy in love.

For her and Mac, it had been love at first sight. Ella had never believed in such things before she'd met Mac, always being a pragmatic person and never one to get carried away with flights of fancy. But, as their gazes had connected in an explosive collision her first day on the job, Ella had begun to fall irrevocably in love. Something about Mac made her forget that she was desperately poor. That she was from the wrong side of the proverbial tracks. That she had no pedigree, no fancy schooling, not even any family to speak of.

From that first day, whenever she was in Mac's presence, Ella would suddenly feel as if she were worthy of his attention. The trappings of poverty would fall away and she was transformed from a poor girl in an unattractive uniform, to a beautiful woman in his eyes.

Yes. She was crazy in love. And love made people do strange things, she'd heard. Well, she would be careful, she promised herself. She wouldn't get hurt. She wouldn't embarrass Mac or his family. She would simply enjoy a few magical moments in his presence, and—when Mac eventually found a suitable woman to marry—she would turn back into the pumpkin she'd always been.

Lifting her eyes, she glanced at the clock on the wall and willed the hands to fly toward twelve. It was amazing how twenty minutes could seem like an eternity, when she was waiting to see Mac.

Many long minutes later, as the various clocks in the mansion struck twelve, Ella found herself standing behind the large fountain in the rose garden. The view from where she stood was fabulous and quite beyond her wildest dreams as a young girl hoping for a different and better future.

It was a beautiful day on a beautiful estate. The huge, Brubaker antebellum mansion was breathtaking in both its style and enormity. Pillars, like sturdy sentinels, guarded the house proper, supporting what looked like acres of veranda on the first and second floors. The long driveway was lined with shade trees and a half dozen other buildings dotted the surrounding area. From where she stood, Ella could clearly see the servants' quarters that housed her cozy room, a giant garage, the pool house, a gazebo, a greenhouse, the stables and the professionally manicured rose gardens in which she stood. It was paradise. Perfect for romance.

Folding her collar up, Ella attempted to give her dowdy uniform a little style. Then she bit her lips then pinched her cheeks and hoped that she looked half as beautiful as Mac made her feel. Filled with eager anticipation, her eyes darted back and forth as she attempted to catch a glimpse of him.

She squealed with surprised delight when she felt Mac's hands steal around her from behind. Pulling her into his arms, he turned her around and hauled her against his chest.

"What took you so long? I've been waiting forever," he growled and nuzzled her on the neck. "You're late."

"I am not," she retorted, teasingly. "You're early." Giggling, she looped her arms around his neck and filled her hands with the thick, honey-colored hair that lay there. "Besides, Bertha was grumpy today and gave me extra chores."

"I'm going to have to see about getting Bertha transferred."

"No!" Ella gasped, glancing at the kitchen window. Seeing Bertha's nose pressed flat against the glass, she tugged Mac farther behind the bush that lay between them and the house. Under no circumstances did Ella want to do anything that could jeopardize her job. "Mac, you mustn't do that. I don't want to get Bertha in trouble. I need this job. I," she said, faltering as a heated stain crept across her cheeks, "I don't have anything else." It was true.

"You have me," Mac murmured, pulling her up close and cupping her face in his hands.

Capturing his hand between her cheek and shoulder, Ella smiled despite her melancholy. For now, yes. For the next few minutes. But in the harsh glare of reality, no. Bertha's words had left their intended mark. A deep sigh shuddered through her body. Having Big Daddy pluck her from the hot and sticky kitchen down at the Rib-O-Rama and give her a position in his own kitchen was a touch of fate that a person such as herself couldn't count on happening more than once in a lifetime. She was earning more money and gaining more experience under Bertha's watchful eye than she ever could have dreamed possible with her limited education.

Just standing here in the garden with Mac was putting all this in jeopardy, she knew, but…there was something so completely irresistible about Mac. She simply couldn't seem to control her emotions when it came to him. A pang of guilt stabbed her heart. Never before had she acted with such carefree, reckless abandon, when it came to her precious employment. She'd learned long ago that a paycheck—no matter how meager—was the difference between a full and an empty stomach.

"Come here," Mac groaned, taking her hand and leading her to the opening of the maze and drawing her inside. The tall hedge would shelter them from prying eyes.

Tilting her chin, Mac angled her mouth beneath his. As his lips settled firmly over hers, he cradled her head in his hands and she shifted her body more firmly into his, snuggling, seeking his strength and his confidence in their relationship. Their passion was voracious, and their kiss greedy and frenzied. They had so little time together, so few stolen moments to revel in each other's embrace, that they attempted to make every second a lasting memory. Hands and mouths moved, explored and searched insatiably.

"Mac," she implored, his name a small whimpering sound, and felt his body quicken in response.

She was lost forever, and she knew it.

Never before had Ella been so carried away by a single

moment, but surprisingly, she suddenly found that she didn't care anymore. She didn't care about Bertha, she didn't care about her job, she didn't care about the callous, unfeeling opinions of others. Of Stormy. Or of Stormy's daughters.

All she cared about was being with Mac. Loving Mac.

Their breathing ragged, she clung ever more tightly to him to keep from falling down. Through the dizzying fog that enveloped her, she could feel the rasp of his beard on her smooth cheeks and lips. She could feel the incredible softness of his golden hair, she could feel the pounding of his heart beneath the solid surface of his broad chest, and she could feel the muscles of his strong arms encircling her waist.

Exploring, touching, kissing and gasping for air and sanity, they stood in the shadows, communicating the love they felt for each other that transcended words and bank accounts and...reality.

"I want you," Mac gasped, gripping her arms and putting her away from his body in an effort to catch his breath. His hands in her hair, he tilted her chin and searched her face with his probing eyes.

"I know. I want you, too," she returned, feeling as if she may die without him.

"No," Mac groaned and kissed her once again, quick and hard on the mouth, "I mean I want you forever. I've never met anyone who makes me feel the way you do. I could conquer the world with you at my side."

"Please, Mac," she sighed raggedly as Bertha's scathing words suddenly reared back and galloped through her mind. As much as she hated to admit, Bertha had a point. Just who did she think she was, standing here, fantasizing about any sort of real future with this man? She touched her fingertip to his lips. "Shh. Don't," she groaned. "It can never be. You don't understand where I come from. I could never fit in with your people.''

"That's crazy. Who cares about my people? I want *you* to fit in with *me*.'' He pulled her back up against his body. "Besides, I'm in love with you. That's all that matters.''

"Oh, Mac,'' she breathed past the growing lump in her throat. He was such a wonderful man. "You don't know what hearing you say that means to me. But—'' her eyes burned, as did her throat "—it's not meant to be.'' Surely she loved him enough to let him go, if she had to.

"Yes. It *is!* Marry me,'' he urged, whispering against her lips and driving all rational thought from her head. "I want you. I want you to marry me and be my wife. The mother of my children.''

Ella stared at him, alternately incredulous with shock and delirious with an unrealistic euphoria. "But…but we've only known each other for two months!'' she sputtered. No, she sternly told her foolishly pounding heart. Marriage wouldn't be fair to either of them, in the long run. She couldn't fall for his reasoning, tempting though it was. A light romance was one thing. A lifelong commitment to a lifestyle she didn't completely understand, was quite another. Still, it was so wonderful to hear him give credibility to her fantasy.

"Who cares? Two weeks, two minutes, two years. I know I love you and I know I will love you forever. No matter what.''

"You're not serious,'' she sighed, wanting desperately to believe, yet afraid at the same time.

"Yes. I am. And I know you love me, too. Look me in the eye and say it's not true.''

Her gaze penetrated his in an unwavering stare, and she bit her lip as tears of futility pricked the backs of her eyes. "I can't,'' she murmured.

"I knew it." He crowed triumphantly and kissed her again. "Marry me, Ella," he demanded.

"I can't," she protested as a small smile tugged her lips at his enthusiastic insistence. "It would be folly."

He ignored her. "Elope with me. Tonight. I can't wait any longer. I need you. I want you. Please, Ella, say you will."

"No," she gasped, beginning to buy into the dream. Laughing, her eyes searching his face as she began to consider his words. She was starting to think he was really, truly serious. Oh, but she could never seriously entertain such a wild idea. Could she? Her heart fluttered wildly. Did she dare? Amusement bubbled within her throat when she considered the look on old Bertha's sour face when the old girl heard the news.

And Stormy? The woman's vicious words still burned like a poison dart in the corner of her mind. *"You'll never amount to a hill of beans, just like your pathetic father."*

She took a calming breath. Stormy was wrong. But even so, could she honestly consider marriage? To a Brubaker?

"Your family would never get over the shock."

"My family wants me to get married."

"But not to the *kitchen* help, Mac! I would never be able to make you proud with your elite social circle. That would be like Bertha marrying your father! Don't you see, it would never work!"

"That's because my father is already married." Mac chuckled, exasperated with her logic. "Ella my love, listen, you make *me* proud. That's *all* that matters."

When he said it so vehemently, she could almost believe it. For a moment, in her heart of hearts, she allowed herself the luxury of dancing on clouds, and pushing the consequences of a rash decision out of her mind. Listening to

Mac this way made her believe that anything was possible. Made her believe in fairy tales.

"I'm coming to your room this evening as soon as you get off work. I want you dressed and ready to go."

Breathless she gripped his upper arms for support. He was serious. "Where are we going?" she asked, stupefied by this whirlwind conversation. She glanced at her watch. Nearly an hour had slipped by. She was already late getting back to the kitchen. Bertha would read her the riot act for sure.

"To the county courthouse. We are getting married." It wasn't a request anymore. It was an order. "There are a few people down there who owe me some big favors. I'll make all the arrangements for us this afternoon."

"But...but...won't your parents be devastated? I mean, your folks are still crowing about your older brother's lavish wedding and that was over a month ago. I know that they would be hurt if you didn't tell them what you're planning to do."

"Ella, I'm a big boy. If I want to elope, I will. They will simply have to learn to live with it, and accept my decision. It's my life. My business." At her dubious expression, he touched his finger to her nose, then let it trail to her lips. "Hey, listen to me. I want you all to myself for a while. I've waited for two torturous months to spend more than a moment or two alone with you. I don't want to have to wait another year while my family rallies around picking out wedding invitations and caterers and all that froufrou stuff."

"But I don't have anything to wear," she protested weakly, fearing somehow that this was the least of her troubles, but unable to think of another reason as to why this might not work. Certainly Mac seemed to feel that there was no problem that he couldn't handle. Angling her chin, she admired the glint of determination in his eyes. He was such a strong man. He had a way of making her feel that she could conquer any travail that life might toss their way.

"Listen," he groaned, allowing his forehead to thump lightly against hers. "I wouldn't care if you met me at the altar in a sackcloth. However, we can stop and get you a dress before the ceremony. Hell, we can stop and get you an entire trousseau, if you like. Just say you'll marry me tonight. I can't wait any longer. Tell me you want this as much as I do."

Ella, swept away by the thrill of this exquisite dream, simply nodded. Struck dumb, her voice had failed her completely. Before she could squeak out another protest, Mac kissed her again then sent her back to the scowling Bertha.

Stretching languidly, Ella's eyes slowly fluttered open. The predawn light of day was just beginning to filter through the curtains and slanted softly over the bed she shared with her new husband. Not wanting to disturb him as he lay sleeping, she shifted ever so slightly and studied Mac's slumbering features.

She would be forever grateful to him for insisting that they elope yesterday. Never would she have had the courage to do something so rash, so impetuous, so...so full of disregard for social distinction and protocol. But, here she was, secreted away, in the quaint Brubaker guest cottage like something out of a...well, out of a fairy tale.

After a dizzying ceremony down at the county courthouse—where a good friend of the family had put a rush order on the legal particulars of which she knew very little—Mac had swept her into a waiting limousine and they'd dined at an elegant restaurant on the outskirts of Dallas. Although the four-star establishment was one of the finest in the country, the fabulous view and surroundings hadn't mattered one whit to the starry-eyed Ella. All evening, she'd been living in an enchanted dream, alternately fearsomely nervous and wildly excited. Their dinner went largely untouched as she and her new husband had gazed into each other's eyes and toyed with their silverware.

Then, after what seemed like an eternity to Ella, Mac signed for their bill, summoned the car and took her back to the ranch for their first night together as a married couple.

The Brubaker guest house was a delightful cottage, situated in a secluded grove, down near the entrance to the mile-long, tree-lined driveway. No one would find them there, Mac had assured her as he'd swept her into his arms, carried her over the threshold and kicked shut the front door with the heel of his boot. Striding down the hallway he headed for the master suite and, unable to wait another moment, took his new wife to bed.

And now, the morning after a glorious wedding night spent making love, Ella was more hopelessly in love with Mac than she ever thought possible. For, had she known how thrilling a night in his arms would actually be, she'd have agreed to elope with him without protest. In fact, she may have suggested it herself, she thought with a lazy, sated smile.

Oh, she was an incredibly lucky woman, she thought, her heart swelling with pride and passion for this man as she watched his strongly chiseled lips puff softly, his bare chest rising and falling with the deep breath of slumber. The white linen sheets were twisted around his lower torso, and his hairy leg, flung possessively over her smooth ones, was a sweet contrast in the dappled morning light. Her throat constricted at the touching sight, and she felt her eyes grow misty.

With two simple words he'd taken her as his lifetime

partner and elevated her from the status of mere servant to that of family member. *I do*. Were there any more awe-inspiring words in the English language?

Ella didn't think so. If there were, no one had ever taken the time nor effort to say them to her. Her abysmal child-hood with Stormy had left her with precious little self-confidence. Had her own parents lived to raise her, Ella was sure her life would have been vastly different. How-ever, such was not to be her fate and luckily none of that mattered anymore. Her shoddy existence as a hardworking girl in rags was a thing of the past. Nothing but a hazy memory.

She was Ella Brubaker now. A woman of substance. She had a loving husband, a large, affectionate family whom she adored, food for her stomach, clothes to keep her warm and a clean, comfortable place to lay her head for the rest of her life.

Moving over his body, Ella's gaze came to rest on his face—so handsome in repose—and silently gave thanks for such a wonderful man. Certainly she didn't feel that she'd done anything special to deserve a husband of Mac's con-siderable wealth and position in life, but she wouldn't ques-tion her good fortune.

And her good fortune didn't stop there, she mused, studying the way his heavily fringed lashes cast a subtle shadow across his sculpted cheekbones. He was such an amazingly handsome man. Any number of beautiful, well-bred women could be lying here beside him as his wife, and yet, he'd chosen her, a simple girl with a plain and impoverished background. Would wonders never cease?

As if he could sense her watching him, Mac took a deep breath and, slowly coming to consciousness, slanted a sat-isfied look at her.

"What are you doing?" he murmured sleepily, snaking

an arm around her waist and drawing her back into the curve of his body.

"Watching you sleep," she admitted with a smile.

"That must be interesting." His tone was playfully droll.

"Mmm. Very."

"I know something much, *much* more interesting that we could be doing," he teased, propping himself up on an elbow and looking down into her face.

Feigning innocence, Ella arched a brow. "And, what would that be?"

"I think you know perfectly well, Mrs. Brubaker," he growled and rained a trail of kisses from her ear to the hollow of her throat and beyond as he pulled her beneath his body. Another hour melted away unnoticed by the pair.

After a heavenly morning spent learning much more about the wonders and secrets of each other, Mac, a relaxed expression on his face and resting comfortably on his elbow at her side, leaned over and kissed the tip of Ella's nose.

"I've been thinking…" he began.

"Oh, no." Ella giggled and pulled the sheet up under her chin. "Not again."

"You are a very naughty girl," Mac chuckled, "but for one—very brief, mind you—moment, I really was thinking of something other than your ravishing body."

Thrusting her lower lip out, Ella pretended to pout. "So, what is this other thing that has captured your interest?"

"Well," he sighed. Pondering a moment, he chose his words with care. "I've been thinking that we should keep our marriage secret for a while."

Suddenly assailed with a jolt of her old self-doubt, Ella leaned slightly away from him and folded her arms across her middle in a defensive posture.

"Oh? Why?" she asked attempting to keep her tone light even as she dreaded the answer. Was he having second thoughts? Now that they'd satisfied their passion, would he regret his impulse to marry someone from her lowly station in life? Her stomach clenched uncomfortably as she regarded him.

His voice became soothing. Silky. "No particular reason. It's just that I would like to enjoy some privacy with my new bride. I don't want to have to listen to a lot of haranguing about why we eloped without benefit of a big Brubaker wedding."

"Oh." Well, that was all right, she thought, with a light lift of her shoulders. She couldn't blame him for wanting to wait a little while before breaking this rather...startling news to his family. Could she? Smiling, she attempted to shake off the funk that had settled over her previously buoyant mood. "I suppose you have a point. And I know I have to get back to the kitchen."

"Oh, honey, you don't have to go back to the kitchen," Mac said, stroking her hair as it lay, free-flowing against the pillow. "I don't want you to have to work at all, if you don't want to. Especially not in the kitchen."

"I can't just not go to work anymore," Ella protested, arching a puzzled brow. "Wouldn't that seem odd, quitting my job, then hanging around waiting for you every day? Bertha would blow her cork for sure and the jig would be up."

"Call in sick," Mac urged, tugging her into the curve of his body. "For a whole week. I will, too."

"Oh right. How would that look, both of us playing hooky for a week?" Ella smiled. "No, Bertha will already wonder where I've been this morning. She has no idea what has happened to me since yesterday. And besides, I wouldn't want to leave Big Daddy without a pastry chef."

"No," Mac mused. "I guess you're right. That wouldn't be such a good idea at this particular juncture. But just as soon as we can hire someone to take your place, I want you out of there.''

Why? Ella wondered as the fingers of doubt began to claw at her heart once again. Was he suddenly realizing that the idea of being married to the kitchen help was not the idyllic future his family had envisioned for him? Absently she twisted the hem of the sheet beneath her chin, unable to dispel the niggling blossoms of worry that were suddenly blooming in that secret corner of her mind. That pragmatic corner that always told her that if something was too good to be true, it usually was just that.

Stormy's voice reverberated in her troubled mind. *"You'll never make it on your own. Not on a maid's salary. And that, my dear, is all you're good for.''*

Agitated, she smiled through her worries at her new husband. He'd vowed for richer or poorer. Was he regretting this vow?

"Don't concern yourself about me. I don't mind working. Really,'' she told him, attempting once again to shove her doubts to the back of her mind. "And Bertha needs the help. Especially today. Your parents are hosting a little tea in the drawing room and I'm serving the pastries. It would seem that some old friends of the family are returning for a visit today.''

"Really?'' Mac wondered aloud. "Who?''

A minxish grin transformed her face. "Your favorite. The Fergusons.''

"Yeesh. I wonder what they're doing back again so soon. Thanks for the warning. I'll come straight home from the office and hide out here with you when you get off work.'' He growled meaningfully into her ear.

"Don't you want to say hello to the Fergusons?'' Ella asked curiously.

"Nope. When Big Daddy and George get to jawing

about the good old days, mere mortals have been known to fall into a catatonic state.'' Mac rubbed Ella's nose with his own as he flung his arm over her hip. ''Besides, I haven't seen him since I was eight or nine years old. He wouldn't know me from Adam.'' His hands roved her hips, exploring her curves, memorizing them. ''You're sure you don't want to stay here and play hooky with me all day? They won't miss me down at the office. I'm the boss. I can call and tell them that something more important has come up.''

''Mac Brubaker, you are truly an insatiable man.''

Patting her on the fanny, he grinned. ''I aim to please.''

''You do,'' she murmured, and glanced at the clock as she wound her arms around his neck. They still had several hours before she had to be at work.

She would play hooky until then.

A long while later, Mac woke to find Ella already gone for the day. As he stretched and yawned, he felt his spirits droop. He wished she was still there, pressed against his body, and not already in the kitchen working under Bertha's eagle eye. She was a conscientious one, his bride was. Mac lay there for a while and longed for her sweet touch. Too bad they weren't laying in a cabana somewhere, watching the waves crash against the beach of a tropical island.

Oh well. He'd been impatient to begin his married life. Soon Ella would be out of the kitchen forever. And, the announcements, the receptions and the honeymoon would all come in good time.

But first, he simply wanted some private, uninterrupted time with the woman who, in two short months, had transformed his life to a little piece of heaven on earth. Glancing at the alarm clock on the nightstand, he did some mental calculations. Eight hours and they would be in each other's arms again.

In the meantime, he thought as he sat up and swung his legs to the floor, he would spend the day down at the office, avoiding the no doubt frenzied reunion between the Fergusons and his parents, and of course, dreaming of Ella.

Little did Mac know, that after a long, impatient day at the office, he would return to find no trace of Ella but a single bedroom slipper.

Chapter Three

Nine long months later

"Why are you in such a blasted hurry?" Mac demanded.

Raking his hands through his hair, he mentally counted to ten as he stared at his father. Big Daddy had no idea what he was asking, and at the moment, Mac had no intention of telling him.

Seated in matching leather wing chairs in front of the library fireplace, the two stubborn opponents faced each other. Neither was willing to give an inch.

"What are you waiting for? The summer is already half over! If you're gonna get married in September like Bru and Penelope did last year, you're gonna have to start plannin' now! They're already married and expectin' a baby any minute. And what are you doin'? Lollygaggin' around!" Exasperated, Big Daddy stared over the top of his appointment book at his son.

Mac groaned, pushed beyond endurance. Leaping to his feet, he planted his hands on his hips and towered over his father. Fortunately, before he could unleash the years of frustration that crowded into his throat, his mother interrupted.

"Mac, darlin', this telegram just came for you," Miss Clarise announced as she gracefully sailed across the highly polished hardwood of the library floor.

She hesitated as she reached her son. The thunderclouds were gathering in the opulent room between Mac and Big Daddy. It was obvious to anyone who entered that the two were embroiled in a heated discussion.

"*Poor Holly,*" she murmured under her breath. Their old friends George and Trudy Ferguson's lovely daughter had been waiting out on the front lawn for Mac for quite a while now. They'd been in the middle of a croquet game when Big Daddy had summoned Mac to the library. Miss Clarise extended the yellow missive toward her son. "Here you go, sweetheart."

"*Telegram?*" Big Daddy thundered. "Who would send a telegram in this day and age of computers and fax machines?"

Rolling his eyes, Mac shook his head. Grateful for the reprieve from his father's nonstop harangue, he ripped open the telegram and began to read. As his eyes moved over the words printed there, his demeanor changed in a way that was nearly electric in its intensity.

Miss Clarise and Big Daddy exchanged curious glances.

Mac's mouth dropped and his eyes glazed over. Then, his jaw hardened and his eyes became steely as the words finally penetrated his muddled brain.

They'd found Ella.

"Well?" Big Daddy demanded, glancing back and forth

with keen interest between his wife and son. "Who's it from?"

Dazed from the many emotions that swirled through his mind, Mac crumpled the telegram he'd been reading. Stuffing it into his pocket, he strode across the room to the door where he paused and stared unseeingly at his parents.

So much had happened in the last nine hellish months since Ella's mysterious disappearance the day after their wedding. The words on the telegram suddenly transported him back in his mind to that agonizing evening. The pain was still rapier sharp.

After he'd returned from the office, he had rushed home to the guest house to sweep his new bride into his arms, only to discover that Ella wasn't there. Neither was the small satchel that held all of her meager worldly possessions.

No, the only thing left of Ella McCloskey Brubaker was the cryptic note propped on the bedroom pillow, the subtle scent of her floral cologne and a single bedroom slipper he'd found tucked between his boots under the guest house bed.

Hurt and confused, Mac had searched the note that instructed him not to go after her for some clues to her whereabouts, but there were none. Scrawled in her delicate hand, the instructions were simply that he not follow her. Giving no real explanation, the note had curtly stated that she regretted her impulsive decision to marry him and that she wanted out. In no uncertain terms. Out of their marriage. Out of her job.

Out of his life.

Many times he'd picked up the phone to call the police, but something about the note, written in her familiar handwriting made him know that she'd left of her own accord.

The police couldn't force her into a marriage she didn't want, no matter how much he wished they could.

The divorce papers had arrived soon after, needing only his signature to complete the dissolution of their marriage. Ella hadn't wasted any time with the legalities, he'd noted, stunned at her bold and unfeeling behavior. Refusing to put his signature on a document that went against everything he believed when he'd pledged his life to her, Mac had crumpled the divorce decree into a ball and hurled it savagely into the fireplace.

If she wanted a damned divorce, let her come and get it, he thought, boiling with fury.

Unfortunately, much to Mac's devastation, he hadn't seen or heard from her again. For the better part of a year now, he'd been numb by the worry and grief and hurt. Deep in his heart, Mac knew that there had to be more to Ella's defection than met the eye. Someday, he aimed to find out what had compelled her to run. Making it his mission in life, he decided he would get to the bottom of this mystery, or die trying. For now, he would bide his time, and wait for the opportunity to see her again.

Whatever had driven her away could be overcome with love. Of that, Mac was sure. His own parents' loving marriage had taught him that time and time again.

In the meantime, not wanting to go into the details of his mistake with his sensitive parents, Mac had remained quiet about his marriage. They'd be hurt to find that he'd gotten married without inviting the whole Brubaker gaggle along for the show. No, confessing that he'd run off to get married only to have his bride turn around and run off after the wedding was more than Mac could confess to his parents. No doubt Big Daddy would have taken it upon himself to call out the cavalry to search for Ella.

For Mac was not the only one devastated by Ella's disappearance.

Mac clearly remembered his father's crestfallen expression when Big Daddy had learned that his favorite pastry chef in the Lone Star State was gone. And, without so much as a backward glance after only two months on the job. It seemed to everyone that the old man would have liked to have broken down and cried.

No. Telling Big Daddy that Ella was "the daughter-in-law that got away" would have been more than the old man could take. Even the stodgy Bertha had seemed surprised and a little dewy eyed at Ella's sudden disappearance.

Gripping the door frame, Mac resurfaced from his reverie and focused on his parents as they stood staring at him, waiting for an explanation. Unfortunately, after months of hovering in limbo, the proper words eluded him. He couldn't tell them. Not yet. Not until he saw Ella for himself. Now that he knew where she was, he might just find the answers he so desperately needed. For a sense of closure, if nothing else. Anxiety coiled his gut into a tangled knot.

Adam Mattheson—the private investigator he'd hired— had finally found Ella. She was less than a hundred miles away. Practically under his nose all this time.

He had to go to her.

Now.

Forgetting his parents in his glassy-eyed single-mindedness, he slapped the palm of his hand against the door casing and, spinning on his heel, bolted out of the room and down the hall.

Big Daddy rushed through the library's twin doors after his son's rapidly retreating form, his brow pulled into a quizzical caterpillar. *"Mac!"* he hollered at the top of his lungs. "Mac! What was in that telegram? And, where are you goin'?"

Mac paused at the hall closet that was situated beneath one end of the massive double staircase. Yanking open the door, he called over his shoulder in a grim voice that echoed over the smooth surface of the black-and-white marble floor. "I have to go."

"Right *now?* But where?"

"On a trip," he muttered, reaching into the closet for the travel bag he'd packed for just such an event. Tucked into its canvas pockets were his toiletries, a few changes of clothes, the terse note Ella had left him and her remaining bedroom slipper. "It's personal. It's an emergency." He spoke distractedly from the interior of the closet. "I have to go now, and I have to go alone. I'll call you in a few days."

"*Days?*"

"Maybe. Maybe weeks."

"*Weeks?*" Big Daddy thundered. "You're leavin' on an emergency trip for several *weeks? Now?* But, what about Holly? What about her parents? What about settin' your weddin' date? What about your responsibilities down at Brubaker International?" Big Daddy demanded as he trotted down the hallway after his son.

"This is more important," he flung over his shoulder.

"What could possibly be more important?" Big Daddy watched incredulously as Mac slammed the closet door and barreled across the expansive columned foyer. "Hey, boy! What the hell do you think you're doin'? Somebody has to run your end of the company!" he shouted. "You can't expect Bru to carry your load because you up and decide to take an unscheduled vacation." Seeing that his scathing diatribe was not having the desired effect, Big Daddy flapped his stubby arms in frustrated circles, sending the fringe of his leather jacket flying. "Well, at least tell me how I can get a hold of you."

"I don't know. I'll let you know when I find out." Mac's clipped words grew dim as he reached the leaded-glass front door and, yanking it open, stepped outside. "Expect me when you see me."

"But, but... Now listen here..." Big Daddy sputtered, his jaw slack, his wiry brows now sky-high.

The door slammed with a resounding crash of finality.

From his vantage point behind the intricate panes of leaded glass in the front door, Big Daddy could see his son striding across the lawn toward Holly Ferguson, as she waited for him to resume their game of croquet.

"What in tarnation is goin' on around here?" the older man ranted, pressing his nose to the glass door and taking in the look of shock and surprise that crossed Holly's face, as Mac spoke rapidly to her.

"I don't know, Big Daddy," Miss Clarise murmured as she stepped up behind her husband, "but for once, may I suggest that you keep your nose out of it."

"Like *hell*," Big Daddy roared. Throwing open the front door, he strode purposefully after Mac. He arrived on the lawn just in time to watch, in hang-jawed amazement, as his son grabbed the roll bars of his convertible Jeep and swung himself inside.

Grinding gears as he impatiently floored the gas pedal, Mac spun in a dangerous circle. Again he forced the protesting gears through the box. Then, with a departing nod at the shocked faces that watched from the lawn, he proceeded to tear down the long, tree-lined driveway. A cloud of dust swallowed him as he disappeared from sight.

After a quick confab with the emotional Holly, Big Daddy came stumbling back into the house to face his wife with glazed eyes.

"I just can't believe it! He's really *gone!*"

Puzzled, Miss Clarise tugged Big Daddy into the living room and over to a love seat near the fireplace where she motioned for him to sit down before he fell down.

"Take a deep breath, Big Daddy," she instructed. Fanning his crimson face with her handkerchief, she encouraged him to continue. "Now, tell me. What did Holly say?"

"That poor girl is so beside herself, she can hardly speak. I came back inside to give her a moment alone to collect herself. All I was able to gather through her uncontrollable sobbin' was that Mac didn't give her any more clues than he gave us! *Personal emergency. Bah.* Well I want to know, what in blue blazes is so personal that he can't share it with his fiancée? And, how could he just take off like that, with no notice or preplannin'?"

"I don't rightly know," Miss Clarise murmured. Sinking into the love seat next to her sputtering husband, she allowed her gaze to stray out the window. Holly cut a forlorn figure, standing alone in the middle of the lawn, her croquet mallet dangling uselessly from her fingertips. It was a wrenching sight. "What do you suppose was in the telegram that upset him so?"

"That's the mystery, sugar doll," Big Daddy muttered, flopping tragically back on the seat. He passed a weary hand over his leathery face. "It looks like a case of cold feet to me. Plain and simple. Oh, I don't feel good about this. I don't feel good about this at all. What am I gonna tell George?"

Miss Clarise *tsked* thoughtfully. "Now, Big Daddy, before you go and make yourself sick, perhaps we should think about giving Mac the benefit of the doubt."

"What benefit of the doubt? What could possibly take

him away from sweet little Holly for several weeks, and right before we started to plan their weddin'?"

"I have to admit, that doesn't sound at all like Mac," Miss Clarise mused. "Such terrible manners are not his usual style, to be sure."

"Maybe we pushed him too hard to set a weddin' date, and he finally snapped," the tiny patriarch lamented. "The boys are always tellin' me I push 'em too hard."

Miss Clarise lifted a knowing brow.

"Well," Big Daddy harrumphed at last, "at least Buck is still here. Maybe he can entertain Miss Holly while we wait for Mac to return."

Head whirling, Mac checked his watch for the umpteenth time as he sped down the highway toward the address in the telegram. It wouldn't be long now. In less than half an hour, he would arrive in the small town where Ella had most recently settled.

Dogleg, Texas.

Mac snorted. *Dogleg.*

"Yeah," he muttered sarcastically under his breath. "Sounds like a real destination point."

During the hour and a half since he'd received the telegram, Mac had traveled over in his mind—as his wheels had traveled over the highway—some of the events that had transpired since he'd seen her last.

So much water had passed under the bridge. So much hurt. So much pain. His trust in the woman he'd thought he'd known so well had been completely shattered. The woman he'd loved more than life itself. How could Ella have played him for a fool this way? What kind of sadistic pleasure had she gotten from that game? he wondered, torturing himself for the millionth time with these agonizing questions. It wasn't as if she'd tried to extort any money from him, or his family. At least not yet.

The muscles between his shoulders tightened automatically and he shrugged to lessen the tension. Shifting to a more comfortable position in his seat he, at the same time, shifted to a more comfortable train of thought.

Allowing himself a small self-deprecating grin, he wondered what Holly must be thinking by now. Poor kid. He'd really left her holding the bag out there on the lawn. He'd owe her one when he got home. She'd been such a good sport all summer. This afternoon as he'd been leaving, he knew his revelation about his marriage to Ella had come as a shock to Holly. However, once she'd understood his predicament, she had agreed to continue to carry on their pseudoengagement for a while longer. She would keep his secret in order to buy him some time to go to Ella.

Then, as he'd given Holly a brotherly peck goodbye on the cheek, she'd burst out laughing. Her bubbling mirth still rang in his ears as she had literally howled at his retreating Jeep. Weakly she'd waved goodbye, her shoulders bobbing with her glee and tears of laughter streaming down her face.

Mac's grin widened a touch and he flexed his hands on the steering wheel. He really liked Holly. Not enough to marry her of course, but as far as platonic women friends went, he could use a few more just like her. She was loyal. He appreciated that in a woman. The muscles in his jaw clenched.

After Ella had left—and not knowing that Mac had already married—Big Daddy had invited Holly to come spend the summer and hopefully hit it off with Mac. Depressed and despondent over Ella's betrayal, Mac had listlessly gone along with his father's wishes that he play host to this longtime friend of the family. It was certainly easier than having to discuss his debacle of a marriage to the young beauty from the kitchen with everyone. Besides, he had reasoned, if he feigned interest in Holly, it would buy him some time to search for Ella.

Much to his eternal relief, Holly had loved the idea of a pretend romance, as she had no more desire to become engaged than Mac. They'd both gone along with the arranged engagement their parents had foisted upon them, knowing that there would never be a marriage. And brilliant or not, Mac and Holly had hoped this practical joke at their parents' expense would keep the meddling foursome off their respective backs.

Hiding out under this guise with Holly had worked out perfectly for Mac. He was in no mood to socialize civilly with the numerous eligible ladies his father was wont to parade out to the house. In fact, Mac knew he would never be able to pull himself out of his dark pit of emotion until he found Ella and discovered why she'd run.

Luckily for him, the renegade Holly had been the perfect cover. Holly hadn't delved into his reasons for not wanting to get married, and Mac hadn't volunteered. The fewer people who knew he was already married, the better. In fact, come to think of it, he hadn't told a soul about his marriage to Ella till he'd confessed to Holly just now.

The lines of the highway had become nothing but a blur as he reflected on the last months of that summer. His and Holly's harebrained engagement charade would be ending soon. It couldn't go on forever. Especially not now that he was on the verge of finally seeing Ella again.

His stomach tightened at the thought.

Just beyond Mac's windshield, the desolate countryside flew by. Dotted here and there on overgrown parcels of property, were broken-down shanties littered with yard debris. Obviously, Mac mused, the little town of Dogleg was suffering from more than one economic setback. A lopsided sign announcing that he was now Entering Dogleg, Population 142 teetered at the edge of the ditch and requested that he drive carefully and enjoy his stay.

So, Ella had chosen Dogleg over him and the life he offered. Shaking his head, he could scarcely believe it. *Why?* Had he really been that wrong about her? While it was true they hadn't known each other that long, he'd believed they'd connected on a level that transcended their difference in background. He'd believed they'd connected on a level that bound them together for eternity. And, he'd thought he'd proved that to her by vowing to love her forever, no matter what. Now...well, now he wasn't sure how he felt anymore. But it was certainly not the roaring happiness that filled his gut those first two months after Big Daddy had hired her.

His ruminations shifted to the first time he'd ever kissed Ella McCloskey.

It had taken him nearly a week to screw up enough nerve to ask her out for a date and much to his relief and joy, she'd immediately said yes. Of course, after their date, it felt to Mac as if it had taken another eternity to screw up enough nerve to kiss her good-night. But when he finally had, it was well worth the torture of the wait.

And, man oh man, she was perfect for him, he'd thought on that magical fall night. Perfect. In every way. That much was crystal clear to him even though they came from backgrounds that were galaxies apart. The way their bodies melded so perfectly together when he drew her into his embrace at the end of the evening, was only one of a multitude of ways in which they suited each other.

Once they'd reached the shadowed corner of the servants' quarters porch, Mac could wait no longer and had cupped her cheeks in his hands and lifted her face to his.

"I had a wonderful time, tonight," he'd murmured, his lips nearly touching hers.

"You did?" she breathed, as if she could scarcely believe that a little kitchen servant such as herself could hold his interest for more than a moment or two.

"Quite possibly the best evening in my entire life."

"Oh," she'd replied, "I've seen better movies."

"I'm not referring to the movie." His gaze locked on her emerald eyes. "Or the dinner, for that matter."

"You're not?"

"No."

"Oh." She'd lowered her gaze to his mouth. "Then," she asked, as if unable to help herself, "what?"

"You."

"Oh." The word was warm and sweet against his flesh.

When his mouth finally found hers, she'd tilted her head back and responded eagerly. Mac thought his heart had expanded such that the air was forced forever from his lungs. He couldn't breathe. But it didn't matter anymore. He could live the rest of his life on Ella's kiss alone. Seconds slipped away, then a minute, then more as he lost himself in her.

When his kiss became ravenous, her response was eager. Curious. Innocent.

Breathtaking.

Any momentary shyness she may have suffered before his lips touched hers, drifted away on the autumn breezes as Ella lifted her arms and twined them around his neck. She'd pulled him closer and he'd more than willingly complied, pressing her into the side of the wall and threading his hands into her thick, wonderful, silky blond hair.

The harvest moon hung low in the sky, bathing them in its luminous glow. Off in the distance an owl hooted and was echoed by the even more distant cry of a coyote. Only the stars were there to witness as they clung together, discovering the other half of their respective souls in each other.

When their first kiss had ended, their lips parted, but remained only a whisper away. His hands rested loosely at her waist and their breathing was strident. And, when he'd opened his eyes, he'd found a reflection of his own passion on her sweet face and known then and there that he would someday ask her to be his wife. Someday soon.

Disoriented, Mac blinked himself back to the present.

Little had he known—his thoughts grim as he came to a stop at the only four-way traffic light in the flea-bitten, broken-down town of Dogleg—that the day after she became his wife, Ella McCloskey Brubaker would disappear from his life without a trace.

Until now.

Reaching into his pocket, he extracted the crumpled telegram and studied it for the address where Adam Mattheson, P.I. claimed she now worked. Hell, it couldn't be *that* hard to find her in this pathetic excuse for a town, he thought, lowering his sunglasses on his nose and glancing disdainfully around. There were only a handful of buildings, and only half of those weren't abandoned.

It was then that he saw it. Midway down the street a sign, whose painted letters were blistered and peeling, proclaimed that this was Uncle Clyde's Diner and Pie Shoppe. Another sign in the window boasted fine dining and some of the best pastries in this part of the country.

Yep, Mac thought uneasily as he spotted Mattheson's car parked inconspicuously down the street, this must be the place.

Chapter Four

"Holy-moly!" Clyde Johnson rasped excitedly and ran a gnarled finger over the silver stubble on his jaw. "The G-men are comin', Babe!"

"G-men?" Ella wondered aloud. She dabbed at the damp tendrils of hair that framed her face with the back of her wrist. Glancing up from her stool at the baking table, she arched a curious brow at the wiry geezer who was her latest employer. It was incredibly hot back here in the acrid kitchen of Uncle Clyde's Diner and Pie Shoppe. Stale air hung oppressively in the dilapidated room, as the overhead fan had ceased to work years ago. It was a far cry from the modern convenience of the Brubaker kitchen. At times like this, Ella found herself almost missing Bertha.

"Government men! Revenuers! The *feds!*" Clyde, puffing and wheezing from years of smoking his hand-rolled cigarettes, rattled the paper and pointed at the headline. "Says here they're cracking down on small business owners like me for tax evasion. *Dad-burned sons of guns!*" he shouted, his weathered face scrunching into a murderous mass of wrinkles. Silver hair that hadn't seen a barber in far too long sprouted from his balding pate in unruly wisps and his teeth—the ones that were left—were crooked and yellowed. Puffed and sagging bags framed his faded cornflower blue eyes, which, at the moment, were currently sparking with outrage.

"The feds?" Ella frowned. Sometimes it was hard to follow the crusty Clyde.

"Yes, the feds!" he ranted. "Those snake-bellied sidewinders like to sneak around spyin' on the little guy. One little white lie on the tax forms and the next thing you know, they'll come after ya. Well, they're not gonna take my baby!" he declared, referring to his precious restaurant. "There are laws to protect common folks like me." Turning in an unwieldy fashion on his bum leg, he limped over to the counter. "I got an old law book of Martha's—God rest her soul—layin' around here somewhere," he muttered and, tossing the newspaper onto the baking table, began to yank open the kitchen's various junk drawers and rummaged furiously around.

"What are you worried about, Clyde?" Ella frowned.

"You, Babe!" Pausing in his frenzied search, he squinted at her. "*You!* And of course, my sweet little baby diner."

"Me?" Puzzled, she studied the concern that burned in his bloodshot eyes. "Why are you worried about me?"

"Mostly cuz I ain't been declarin' nothin' on you, being that I only give you a room and a few bucks in cash here and there for your labor."

"Clyde!" she gasped.

"Well, it just didn't seem like that big of a deal. But, accordin' to this here—" he viciously whacked the paper "—it's against the dad-blamed law."

"Oh, Clyde." Exhaling heavily, Ella shook her head.

The last thing she wanted to do was get Clyde into trouble with the law. She owed Clyde more than words could tell, especially being that he'd saved her from starvation not so very long ago. Clyde had hired Ella when she'd been destitute and desperate. The arrangement had worked out well for them both as his beloved wife, Martha, had gone to her reward several years back and Clyde needed the kitchen help.

Like Big Daddy before him, it had taken Clyde only one bite of her peach cobbler for him to hire her on the spot. He could only offer a bit of cash, and since she'd had no place to live, he'd given her one of the small studios in the ramshackle apartment building he ran—and lived in—over the diner. It wasn't the Ritz, but Ella had been grateful for a little place to call home after so many days on the run.

"Oh, Clyde," Ella murmured and held out her hand for the paper. "Here, let me see." They were between shifts and could take a moment to enjoy the quiet of the empty diner.

"See for yourself, if ya don't believe me," Clyde groused and pushed the paper across the table. "I'm tellin' ya there's lotsa stuff that's illegal in this country that don't make no sense." Discovering Martha's old law book under a stack of tattered cookbooks, Clyde dropped it on the table. "Looky here, Babe. Martha always kept this around. Just in case…of…you know…" his mutterings dwindled as he clumsily thumbed through the musty pages. "Hmm."

While he searched, Ella perused the newspaper article he'd been reading. Sure enough, the government had representatives in the area, cracking down on tax evasion among certain small business owners. It was an interesting article, but as far as Ella could tell, Clyde was making his usual mountain out of the proverbial molehill.

"Hey, Babe," Clyde cackled as he searched for the section on laws in the Lone Star State, "did you know it was illegal in New Jersey to slurp your soup?"

"No," Ella replied with a wan smile, her eyes moving over the newspaper as she caught up on the local gossip.

"Yeah, I 'spect I can have half this place under arrest on any given night," he chortled. "Says here, in Canada, it's illegal to board a plane while it's in flight. Hmm. Now don't that beat all," Clyde mused aloud. "In Oregon, it's illegal to require a dead person to serve on a jury, and in Nevada, funeral directors cannot use obscene language in the presence of a dead person." Raspy laughter filled the air over that one.

"Mmm-hmm." As Ella perused the newsprint, something familiar caught her eye on the page opposite Clyde's G-man story.

Something that irrevocably drew her gaze.

Something that had her heart suddenly pounding. Then stopping. Then pounding again. Her breath came in shallow pants as she fought to keep from slipping off her stool.

It was Mac.

Right there, looking back at her, his chiseled lips only half smiling, his eyes vacant of their usual warmth.

Brubaker/Ferguson Nuptials Slated, the caption read.

Mac was getting married.

Clutching her failing heart, Ella leaned forward in her seat at the rickety baking table. Through the spots that swam before her eyes, she stared dazedly at the social section of the newspaper that was spread before her. She should have expected...but she didn't think...

"Boy howdy. Says here, in Washington, it's illegal to pretend your parents are rich. If that ain't the goofiest law I ever heard of, I don't know what is," Clyde harrumphed. "Ya gotta wonder what was goin' through some yahoo's mind when they put that one in the books. But ya know, Babe... Now that gives me an idea.''

The wheels continued to turn in Clyde's mind as Ella's world slowly crumbled.

Clyde cackled. "Pretty gol-danged good idea, really.''

Ella blinked. It was there in black-and-white. Mac Brubaker was getting married.

Thoughtfully Clyde reached up and scratched his silver whiskers. "Listen to this, Babe. I know for sure that I don't have to claim no room and board I'd give a wife. My Martha never claimed the mad money I gave her...''

Ella lifted the back of her hand to her temple in an effort to cool the sudden fire in her head. Something was buzzing. Or howling. Or crying. Was it her? Clyde's voice droned on in the background as he discussed his findings in his nutty law book. Waves of burning nausea rose from her belly and into her throat. She clasped her other hand across her mouth, swallowed against the bitter taste of bile and waited for the light-headed feelings to subside. She was going to faint. She was going to be sick. No. She was simply going to die.

Mac was getting married.

There would never be any going back now.

Never. Not for any reason.

Lifting her eyes, she stared out the dingy window into the vacant street. Heat shimmered on the surface of the pavement, giving her dazed thoughts an even more dreamlike quality. He was going on without her. Just as she'd always known and hoped he would. She simply hadn't known it would be so soon.

"Laws don't say nothing 'bout a man givin' the wife some mad money. Nope. Never heard of anyone declarin' the petty cash. Lord knows that's all I pay you," he said rationalizing.

Not registering Clyde's gravelly mutterings, she refocused on the announcement, morbid curiosity forcing her eyes back to the staggering article.

Pictured beneath the Ferguson and Brubaker headline, was her beloved Mac and his intended, the beautiful Holly Ferguson, socialite daughter of the wealthy George and Trudy Ferguson. Leaning into the crook of his arm, Holly wore a Cheshire smile and looked for all the world like the cat that had roped and hog-tied the canary.

A wet spot darkened the surface of the paper. Then another. And another. Absently Ella swiped at the damp circles, wondering where they'd come from, until she realized her cheeks were streaming with tears. Slowly, ever so slowly, she extended her elbows across the rough surface of her crooked baking table. Lowering her head into her hands the floodgates opened and Ella allowed the grief she'd been holding at bay to finally overtake her. Great sobs shook her slender shoulders and a keening wail rose in her throat as she gave vent to the misery that had welled in her heart for so many months.

Stunned by her uncharacteristic display of emotion, Clyde stopped talking and stared at Ella.

"Aw now, honey," he cajoled, his pliant face knotting into a wad of concern as he thumped in his bandy-legged hitch around the baking table. "Now don't you concern yourself none. It ain't your fault that I didn't fill out them tax forms as honest as I coulda. Besides, maybe them scalawag feds won't even get to old Uncle Clyde's Diner and Pie Shoppe." Awkwardly he patted her back as her haunting cries of anguish echoed throughout the dining room. "Hush now, honey, I got us a plan."

"I...I'm s...s...sorry, Clyde," she stammered brokenly, unable to tell him at the moment, the source of her sorrow. Her breathing was jerky, racking her body as she fought for control. Slumped pathetically across the table's top, the despair overtook her again for a moment.

"Now, honey girl, you ain't got nothin' to be sorry for."

"Y...yes," she blubbered. Her throat constricted and she shut her eyes, temporarily unable to continue.

Yes, she wanted to scream. She had a whole hell of a lot to be sorry for. Mac had found a new love. How could life go on? She felt disoriented, lost in the surroundings of the familiar kitchen.

Distant sounds of the town—a neighbor's shout of greeting, the bark of a stray dog, the backfire of a tractor's engine—filtered into the diner, but she didn't hear.

It was all for the best, she knew.

So why did she feel as if she were about ready to die? Because she still desperately loved him. With all her heart, she would care about and yes, love Mac Brubaker until the day she died. Which, if the way she felt at the moment was any indication, would be today.

"Listen, Babe," Clyde urged, bobbing awkwardly at her shoulder, his blue eyes bright with his ideas. "I gotta plan that will keep us outta trouble. So, stop fretting now, you hear? Everything's gonna be all right. You just let old Clyde take care of everything, you hear?"

Sniffing, she shot a watery smile at Clyde and fished a handkerchief out of her pocket. Pressing it to her red-rimmed eyes, Ella battled back another jag of self-pity. Yes, eventually she supposed, everything would be all right.

She'd made her bed, she thought stoically, and now she was lying in it. From the moment she'd fallen for Mac, she'd known there would be a price to pay for her love.

She simply hadn't known that the price would be so high.

"See her?"

"Mmm-hmm," Mac answered, slowly lowering the binoculars Adam Mattheson had loaned him. He was stunned. In shock. He simply couldn't believe his eyes.

"Is it her?" Mattheson had joined Mac in his Jeep moments after he'd pulled up to the curb and parked.

"Mmm-hmm." Mac nodded dumbly at Mattheson. It was her, all right. No mistaking that. The thing he couldn't get over, get around, get past was her...condition.

She was pregnant. With child. *Great* with child.

Lifting the binoculars back to his eyes, he watched in a daze as she moved slowly back and forth between the kitchen and the dining room. She was having a baby. Could it be his baby? Myriad emotions whipped through his mind, numbing it with confusion. But his heart suffered no such bewilderment. Only longing. Oh, how he'd missed her. How he yearned for her even still. After everything.

But, even as his heart cried out to her, he was still suffering from so much pain. Anger. As relieved as he was to have found her safe and sound, he was also not at all certain of his undying love for her anymore. She had hurt him deeply and now...now he discovered that she was about to have a child.

His child?

Or another man's?

Either scenario made him absolutely blind with rage. His heart was pounding, even as it was breaking all over again. If it was his baby, how could she rob him of the wonder and joy of his firstborn? And, if it wasn't his baby... Well, he didn't want to ponder that too thoroughly at this stage of the game.

Not when he was so blasted furious.

Why hadn't she felt the same level of commitment to their marriage? he wondered, watching her sweet, trustworthy face through the magnified image in the binoculars.

How could she have just up and disappeared the way she did? What had happened between the time they lay entwined in each other's arms the morning after their wedding, and the time she decided to run?

Well, he thought, a grim muscle jumping in his jaw, now that he knew where she was, he would find out what happened. He wanted answers, and dammit, he would get answers.

As these age-old questions assaulted Mac, he could feel Mattheson's eyes regarding him with sympathy.

"Mac, the fact that she's working for room and board and a little cash is why it took so long to find her. The usual routes such as social security were closed to us." Matheson paused and pushed his dark glasses a little farther up on his nose. "Listen, buddy, as much as I hate to say this, the fact of the matter is, most missing people are missing because they want to be."

"Yeah," Mac answered, feeling as if he'd taken yet another hit to the solar plexus. "That much I've gathered."

His eyes strayed over the diner's exterior. It was amazing that this sorry excuse for a building hadn't been condemned years ago. The old-style square Western facade was missing more siding than it sported. Here and there, ragged tar paper clung to the silvery boards beneath. Blistered and peeling, the paint hung in dirty strips from the eaves and trim, and the roof, crooked as the dreary town's name, sagged around a crumbling brick chimney. On the second story, it appeared that someone had tried to make the place a little more homey and appealing by hanging some cheerful curtains in the windows. The incongruity was pathetic.

And Ella was in there because she wanted to be. The thought boggled his mind.

"From what I was able to gather, she hasn't told anyone

her real name and doesn't use a last name at all." Mattheson shrugged.

Brubaker, Mac wanted to shout. *Her name is Brubaker.*

"A lot of people do that," Mattheson continued to explain, "when they don't want to be found. So, for whatever reason, she is probably not going to be greeting you with open arms. I'd imagine she'll be pretty surprised to see you."

Mac snorted sarcastically. "Yeah, well, this is a day for surprises now, isn't it?"

"Buck up, Babe, honey. We're gonna have a big crowd tonight," Clyde predicted, peering at her across the kitchen as he sent a spatter of oil dancing across the grill.

"Yes." Ella nodded woodenly. He said that every night, and every night the same dozen regulars came in for the same steaks and burger baskets. Blinking rapidly, she took a deep breath and squared her shoulders in an attempt to stem the tide of emotion that always accompanied thoughts of Mac. In the past nine months, she'd perfected the art of masking her sorrow. Forcing a smile that was melancholy at best, Ella began to pull the pies out of the cooler that would be required for that evening's dessert.

The cowbell over the door clanked, signaling the arrival of the first two patrons, Selma and Barney Jessop. Selma would have the burger basket, extra fries. Barney would have the T-bone, medium-well. The grill sizzled as Clyde tossed on their dinner without bothering to take their order. There were never any surprises in this town.

"Hey, Babe," Barney called as the Jessops settled into their red vinyl booth.

As far as he and everyone in Dogleg knew, Ella was the mysterious Babe. No last name. No family. No history. Just Babe, plain and simple.

"Hey, Barney. Selma," Ella returned, hoping her voice sounded brighter than she felt.

The cowbell's continued clanking signaled the arrival of the other regulars. As they arrived, the good citizens of Dogleg took their seats and greeted one another.

"Hey, Clyde," Selma warbled from her seat at the booth. "Better throw another burger on the fire. Looks like we might have some new customers."

"Oh, yeah?"

"Yeah. Couple of new guys sittin' across the street in a fancy rig, and lookin' our way."

"How do you know they're gonna come in here?" Clyde hollered back as he slaved over the stifling heat, flipping this and smashing that with his flashing spatulas.

"Because it 'pears to me as if they're lookin' at us through binoculars."

"*G-Men!*" Clyde exploded, expletives filling the kitchen and nearly singeing the food on the grill. Spatulas clattering, he abandoned his post and hobbled over to the order window. Leaning over the sill, he squinted out the grimy pane of glass that made up the front wall of his establishment. "Dagnabbit," he muttered as nervous beads of perspiration popped out on his forehead. "Waddaya wanna bet it's them blasted G-men I read about in the paper?"

"G-men?" Twisting in her seat, Selma craned her neck to better see.

"Feds," Clyde spat.

"Hmm. Now that you mention it, well, I don't mean to alarm you, Clyde darlin', but they do look sorta official."

"Yep," Barney added helpfully. "One of 'em looks kinda hacked off, if you ask me."

One by one, the dozen or so regulars gathered at the front window to peer through the glass at the G-men. Dogleg hadn't seen this much excitement since the general store had collapsed last spring.

Leaning on her stool, Ella arched forward and strained to see for herself what all the commotion was about. Unfortunately her view was blocked by the growing crowd of curious customers.

Settling gingerly back in her seat, Ella gave up and prepared to help Clyde serve dessert. Soon, after everyone had finished gaping at the strangers, they would expect large slices of apple pie and peach cobbler to complete their meal.

"One of 'em's comin' in," somebody shouted.

Ella shook her head, as the crowd scurried back to their seats and attempted to appear as nonchalant as possible. Methodically she sectioned a cobbler into servings. The cowbell clanked.

"Great weather we're havin'," Barney shouted at no one in particular.

"How 'bout them Oilers," came another's contribution.

"I'd like to talk to the owner," the stranger's voice carried back to the kitchen.

That...*voice.*

The hairs at Ella's nape began to tingle and her stomach clenched. It couldn't be. It simply couldn't be. Once again, it was her imagination running away with her. She was simply going to have to get a handle on her wayward thoughts of Mac if she was going to hang on to her tentative sanity.

Taking a deep breath, she edged off her seat and moved over to the order window. Slowly Ella focused on the stranger and her heart began to thunder. That was no G-man.

The man whose eyes were hidden by dark glasses was none other than her ex-husband.

Mac Brubaker.

Head swimming, heart thundering, knees failing, she ducked quickly out of sight.

"Yeah?" Clyde groused churlishly, sizing up his opponent. "Who wants to know?"

"I'm here looking for someone." There was an edge to Mac's voice that Ella had never heard before.

"Who?" Clyde demanded.

"A woman. Her name's Ella. Ella Brubaker. Or maybe she's going by the name Ella McCloskey."

All pretense at conversation in the diner died as the regulars took in the drama being played out before them.

Clyde gave his wispy gray fringe a vehement shake. "Nobody here goes by that name so, unless you're here to eat somethin', I suggest you go lookin' elsewhere."

With an exceedingly deliberate motion, Mac removed his sunglasses and regarded Clyde. "I'll eat."

Silence reigned as all eyes followed the mysterious G-man to an empty booth, and watched in fascination as he took a seat. Nothing cable TV had to offer that night could have beat the excitement that fairly crackled in the air at Uncle Clyde's Diner and Pie Shoppe at that moment.

Feeling faint, Ella groped for her stool and sank down, gripping the top of her baking table for support. Mind swirling for an escape route, she knew she had to get out of here fast. But how? There were only two exits, and both of those were in full view of the dining room. Besides, how fast could she run? In her condition simply getting on and off the stool was a challenge. Filled with anxiety, her eyes darted quickly around the kitchen. There was nowhere to hide.

Obviously Mac knew that she was in here. What else would bring him to a seedy diner out here in the middle of nowhere, over a hundred miles from home?

Okay, she thought frantically. So. He knew she was here. She would have to face the music any moment now. But that did not mean he had to know the reason why she ran away. Setting her jaw, she shrugged off the wretched, pain-filled memories that had sent her into hiding.

And, considering that he was now engaged to a woman of his social ilk, she decided doggedly, as the illogical hurt rose like a lump of her special sourdough bread in her throat, he did not need to know that this was his baby.

With an agility borne of fear, Ella sprang to her feet and moved as quickly out of Mac's field of vision as she dared. Her mind crowded with terrifying thoughts. How had he found her? Had he somehow heard about the baby? Was he here to take the baby away?

Her heart nearly stopped beating as she considered this horrifying idea. Protectively she wrapped her arms around her swollen midsection. This little child was all she had left of her fairy-tale marriage to her prince. And selfish or not, she wanted to keep her child.

She knew some rich people would have no compunction about taking what they believed to be theirs. Would Mac feel the same way? The idea of him, and the spoiled woman he posed with in the society section of the local papers, raising her baby had raw terror clawing at her throat.

As quickly as his bad leg allowed, Clyde limped back into the kitchen and grasped Ella by the wrist. "He's lookin' for someone named Ella. Would that be you? I'm pretty sure it's one of them G-men, all right, honey, wonderin' why I didn't pay nothin' on ya."

"No, Clyde, listen to me, he's..." Ella urgently whispered her protest, but Clyde was zealous in his effort to protect his interests.

"Yes, he is, honey. But don't you worry none. I gotta

plan from Martha's law book. You just stay in here. I'll get rid of him for ya.''

"That won't be necessary.'' Mac's clipped words startled them both as they huddled together in the corner.

Feeling as if she were a prisoner caught by the spotlight while scaling the wall, Ella lifted her lashes and was stunned by the intense brown gaze that so coolly regarded her from just inside the kitchen's door.

Suddenly it was as if she was back in Bertha's kitchen, waiting with breathless anticipation for his arrival. With shaking hands, she released Clyde's bony arm and nervously tucked a stray strand of hair back into her braid.

As their gazes collided, it was for Ella as if the world fell away, and she hadn't been apart from him for nine minutes, let alone nine months.

And, seemingly against his will, his expression softened into one of yearning.

She had to fight the urge to run to his arms and kiss him with the same carefree abandon that she had the last time she'd seen him the night after their wedding.

Oh, how desperately she'd missed him. More so than she'd ever allowed herself to realize. The months faded away and, as she saw her own raw emotion reflected in his face, Ella was suddenly giddy.

He'd missed her, too. She could sense it.

They stared at each other across the stifling and rundown kitchen, drinking in the sight of each other, hearts pounding, blood pressure soaring, minds whirling.

Ella forgot the hurtful secret that had torn them apart.

Mac forgot her painful betrayal.

And for a brief moment, with longing in their bruised and battered hearts, they basked in the sheer unadulterated joy of being in the same room together once again.

Chapter Five

As she soaked up the ecstasy that simply standing in Mac's presence sent zinging through her soul, a million desperate questions crowded into Ella's mind. How were his parents? His brothers and sister? How was the kitchen? Had they hired someone to take her place? How was Bertha?

How was *he* doing? Had he missed her?

Could he ever forgive her for making a decision that, while momentarily painful, was in his own best interest? Unfortunately Ella knew that she could never give voice to this last question. Some things were better left unspoken.

Wistfully her eyes moved over his face, rememorizing every sweet detail and storing them into the hollow corners of her heart. Someday, she would describe his face to her unborn child and tell of the love that would never die, for a man she couldn't have.

Reaching up, she smoothed her disheveled hair back away from her face, knowing that she must look a perfect wreck. Crying always left her eyes swollen and her cheeks blotchy.

At exactly the same time, as he stood under the light of her hungry emerald gaze, Mac also was filled with burning questions. Devouring her with his eyes he wondered how she had come to live in Dogleg. Why hadn't she given him a reason for leaving their marriage? Had she missed him? Did the sweet expression of longing on her face mean she still cared? Was the baby that grew beneath her breast…his?

He wanted to reach out and tuck the stray strands that framed her pink cheeks back into her braid. Pregnancy suited her. For, if it was possible, she looked more beautiful to him than on the day they'd married. Thundering against his rib cage, his heart pined for the time when he and Ella were the only two people in their world, living on nothing but love. Unfortunately for them both, he thought with a dispirited sigh, those days appeared to be gone forever.

Slowly the sounds of the diner began to intrude on this magical moment—as it hovered suspended in time—between Ella and Mac. And, each of them, remembering their acute anguish, mentally began to pull back. To retreat. To allow the defensive walls to come between them once more.

As Ella stood gazing at Mac through eyes of nostalgia, she reminded herself of the painful discovery that had brought her fairy-tale dance with the prince to the abrupt stroke of midnight.

And Mac, his eyes straying to her burgeoning midsection, remembered the hurt and anxiety she'd put him through for nearly a year now. Again, flames licked deep inside his belly as the coals of anger that were ever-present leapt to life.

The frozen tableau of hunger and dashed dreams was finally—and quite suddenly—thawed by Clyde.

"You'd best state your business, mister," Clyde ordered, drawing his bony frame up to its full five and a half feet. Taking a deep breath, he puffed his scrawny chest and stared bravely at the formidable Mac. "Cuz, if you're thinkin' to cause trouble, you got another think comin'."

A muscle twitched in Mac's jaw as he looked down at Clyde from his considerable height.

"Clyde," Ella murmured placatingly and tugged on his sleeve, "please. I—" her deep-sea gaze locked with Mac's "—don't think he's here to hurt you."

"Babe, I read the papers," the curmudgeonly Clyde exclaimed. Holding up the section he'd been reading on G-men, he unwittingly jabbed at Mac and Holly's engagement picture with an arthritic finger, then brandished the paper overhead. The old man could be as ferocious as a mother bear whenever he felt his precious business threatened. "I know why he's here! It don't take a house to fall on me."

Glassy-eyed, Mac's gaze bounced from the crumpled paper in the old man's hand to the ruddy complexion of his face. The paper? What was in the paper?

Ella's eyes riveted to the wadded newsprint and fixed on the spot where Mac's twisted face peeked at them through the folds.

"Yep," Clyde snorted. "He's here to take my baby away!"

"*Your*...baby?" Blanching, Mac tore his eyes away from the ancient cowpoke that tottered before him and refocused on Ella and the gentle swell beneath her apron.

"Yes!" Clyde cried. "Mine! Not yours, *mine*. I worked hard for this one, and I ain't got it in me to start over again on another one."

"You...don't," Mac deadpanned. Planting his fists on his hips, he fixed his incredulous gaze on the old geezer.

"*No!* Just gettin' this one as far along as it is, nearly killed me."

"It nearly...killed you?"

"Yessir! More'n once! Ain't that right, Babe? But I ain't complainin'. After all, how many men my age are lucky enough to still be as active as me?" Clyde sighed a heartfelt sigh. "My late wife, Martha, knew how difficult startin' up was for me. She knew what I went through and it eventually took its toll on her, God rest her soul." He shot a reverent glance at the ceiling.

Completely stupefied, Mac watched the old goat wrap a protective arm around *his* wife's shoulders.

At least Mac thought Ella was still his wife.

He hadn't signed the divorce papers he'd received from her, so he'd assumed that they were still married. As he looked back and forth between the unlikely pair, he began to have his doubts. When he'd refused to sign, had she run off to the Dominican Republic to get a divorce without his knowledge? And for what? For this geriatric spitfire? Uncertainty closed off his throat.

At this point, he wouldn't put anything past her.

Mac slowly shook his head. "Who the hell *are* you?" he growled, completely dumbfounded.

"Well now, not that it's any of your dad-gummed business, but I'm Clyde Johnson, owner of this establishment. And this here, now, she is, uh—" he gave Ella's shoulder a firm squeeze as he spoke "—is...well, my wife, uh, Babe, er, uh, Johnson."

Ella's eyes widened in surprise.

Having thrown down the gauntlet, Clyde forged full-steam ahead. "I give her mad money, and she don't declare it, if that's why you've come snoopin' around." He narrowed a watery blue eye at Mac. "Cuz, she don't have to, bein' that she's my...my wife. That's the law, buddy boy. I know my rights."

Mac's steely gaze hardened.

"Yep—" Clyde continued to put the finishing touches on his tall tale, to authenticate his claims "—we been married a while now, as you can no doubt figure, bein' that she, er, we're in the family way and all. Which would, of course, explain my tax returns."

Ella closed her eyes hoping to block out the mind-boggling mental picture he painted. Groaning inwardly, she rubbed her throbbing temples with the tips of her fingers. She'd had some low points in her life, but this took the cake.

"That's why we know, you being the sensible man you are, you wouldn't want to take my baby—" reaching behind him, Clyde gave the countertop a loving tap "—away. After all, what's a little mad money between a man and his wife?"

"What the *hell* are you talking about?" Mac demanded. Planting his hands on his hips, he studied this disturbing picture. Something was rotten in Dogleg, that much was obvious. And until he got to the bottom of it, he wasn't leaving. Stoically he fought the urge to drag this aging Banty rooster out into the street and kick his sorry tail feathers around the block a time or two. Luckily the old geezer was saved by the bell.

"I'll get that, Babe," Clyde announced. Narrowing a suspicious glance at Mac, he hobbled back to the phone that rang just outside the kitchen in the soda fountain area. "I'll be right back." It was a threat. "Uncle Clyde's Diner," he barked into the instrument.

"Surely you don't expect me to believe that *he* is your

husband.'' Mac jeered, once the old man was out of ear-shot.

"I don't know why not," Ella retorted, suddenly needing air. Moving over to the grill, she turned off the heat before the food caught fire.

Perhaps Clyde was right. Maybe it was simpler for everyone involved if Mac thought she was married. It would certainly solve a multitude of problems. Even so, Ella hated lying to Mac. She was sick at having to resort to these measures to protect them from themselves. But she was desperate. And desperate times called for desperate measures. The baby chose that moment to kick her, just under her heart, and once again she renewed her quest to cling to her unborn child and at the same time set Mac free to live the life he deserved. She was doing it all for love.

"You mean to tell me that you left our marriage for a life here in Dogleg with...*him?*"

"It's my right to marry whomever I wish."

"How can that be?" Daggers of fury shot from his eyes. "You're still married to me!"

What? Ella's heart stopped beating for a moment. Mac hadn't signed the divorce papers she sent? While it was true that she'd never received the final decree, she'd simply figured that's because she'd moved around so much in the days before Clyde had rescued her. For a moment, confusion clouded her mind.

Coming to her senses, she gave her head a clearing shake.

He must have signed them. After all, she'd seen the headlines announcing the fact that he was already halfway to the altar. No, she thought stoutly, deciding to call him on his bluff, it hadn't taken him very long to get over her and move on to Holly. A picture was worth a thousand words and the pictures in the society section said that Mac's new fiancée was thrilled with him.

He was simply digging for information as to why she'd left so abruptly. But it was the only way she could have done it. Another night in his arms, and she'd never have been able to tear herself away.

Yes, he'd signed the divorce papers all right, she thought with certainty, and he'd moved on to fresh territory in record time. It was a lucky thing, she thought—desperately trying to find the silver lining in this hideous rain cloud— that she had left before she discovered Mac could so easily vow his undying love to another woman.

"Married to you?" she scoffed, doing her best to look insulted. Firm. An impenetrable tower of strength, and not the quivering tower of mush she feared that she appeared. "Not anymore." Picking up the crumpled paper that Clyde had left on the baking table, she tapped it against her fingers. "You've made that perfectly clear."

His face scrunched into a quizzical frown as his eyes darted to the rolled-up sheet of newsprint.

Noting his expression, Ella decided he must not want to discuss his precious fiancée. Well, that was just fine with her. She had no desire to tear her heart out with such a discussion. Wadding the paper, she jammed it into her apron pocket, and studied Mac's scowling face. She would wait for him to admit the truth.

Certainly he'd signed the divorce papers. While it may be true that he was fickle, he wasn't stupid. No Brubaker would ever commit bigamy. They were an upstanding family. That was one of the things about them she admired most. She watched his gaze drop curiously to her stomach, and Ella knew that he was doing some mental arithmetic. Trembling, she waited until he'd finished his inspection and brought those mind-numbing, brown eyes to hers.

Angling his head, he looked at her, his expression grim. "Can you honestly look me in the eye and tell me that that is not my baby?"

So, that's why he was here. For the baby. "I...I... You..." she stammered. Unable to sustain his probing gaze, she glanced back toward Clyde and nodded, even though her heart was breaking. Mac had a new life now. A far better one than he would have had if he'd stuck it out with her. She knew it would only be a matter of time before he ended up deeply resenting her. And the sweet, innocent babe that stretched and rolled in her womb.

"Tell me, Ella," he insisted.

"No, I..." She allowed her gaze to collide once again with his, and the deep velvet brown of his eyes lured her into their magical depths. She had to fight this attraction, she thought dully, lulled by his strong, self-assuredness.

Over the past months, away from his hypnotic presence, she had been able to see things much more clearly than when she was under his spell.

Away from him, she could be much more objective. Mac had never really loved her. She could see that now. It wasn't as if he'd meant to hurt her. It was all simply a big mistake. Infatuation. Lust. A physical attraction that had carried them both away. She was not his kind. Never would be. A relationship between the two of them would never last.

As he studied the panic in her expression, his face softened. "Ella, it's my right to know," he murmured, his Southern Comfort voice bringing back memories that had her knees suddenly failing her.

"No," she breathed, refusing to fall victim to his charms. Suddenly feeling as if she were drowning, Ella knew she had to save herself from the emotions this man brought out in her. "We have nothing more to say to each other."

"How can you *say* that?" he demanded, quickly losing his patience. His voice was sharp, filled with frustration and the pain of unanswered questions. "We have everything to say to each other, Ella. We took sacred vows. Doesn't that mean anything to you?"

Yes. It meant that she had made a terrible mistake. One that she'd been regretting for nine months. "Mac," she sighed, her voice broken, "I'm going to have to ask you to leave now. Clyde is…well, he's…very jealous."

His eyes strayed to Clyde as he rummaged through the junk drawer in search of a sharpened pencil. "I can see that," Mac growled, his voice loaded with derision. Eyes snapping, his gaze shot back to her. "Why did you leave?"

"Babe?" Clyde called, the phone tucked between his whiskery chin and shoulder. "Can you fix a couple quiche lorraines for the ranch hand meetin' up at the Double Star Ranch tomorrow mornin'?"

"Yes," she said, never taking her eyes off Mac.

"How 'bout some of that there croquembouche?"

"Yes."

"Baklava?"

"Yes. And I'll have éclairs and croissants, too."

"Great." Clyde went methodically back to the chicken scratchings on his notepad.

The cowbell above the front door jangled signaling the arrival of another regular diner. "Please, Mac," Ella pleaded, closing her eyes against his beautiful face. "I have to go back to work."

Reaching out, Mac gripped her wrist in his hand, and the jolts that sparked between them could have heated Clyde's grill. "When do you get off? We are going to talk." The grim set to his jaw brooked no argument. "You owe me an explanation, if nothing else."

"Please, Mac…" she beseeched, her voice faltering. She

wished with all her heart that he'd simply get into his Jeep and drive back into his own future—the future he had with the lovely and wealthy Holly Ferguson. Just having him touch her arm this way was slowly and softly killing her.

"Babe," Clyde called uncertainly and covered the mouthpiece to the phone, "everything all right over there?"

"Just fine, uh, Clyde," she assured him, her lip quivering. "Please," she pleaded with Mac, "just leave." *Before I change my mind*, she mentally added, her strength flagging. Casting her gaze to the floor, she battled back yet another flood of tears.

"Fine," Mac spat, finally losing his patience. "But you haven't seen the last of me." Spinning on his heel, he stalked to the door. Cowbell jangling, he savagely yanked it open, then strode across the street to his Jeep.

Later that evening, when her shift had ended, Ella bid the overly protective Clyde a fond good-night and headed home. She'd hoped—albeit masochistically—to see Mac's Jeep still parked out on the street, if only for one final glimpse of his beautiful face. However, when she'd opened the front door to the diner and peered down the street, there was no sign of his shiny black Jeep.

He'd gone.

Back to his own life.

And love.

A bitter lump closed off her throat, making breathing difficult. Mounting the stairs that led to her drab little studio apartment, she let the tears flow. She was such an emotional ninny today, she thought angrily, frustrated with her ridiculous crying jags. With an impatient swipe, she blotted the tears on her cheeks with her handkerchief.

Must be her hormones, she rationalized as she let herself into her room and immediately went about fixing herself a hot cup of tea. That would have her sleeping like a baby in no time, she decided, then grimaced tiredly at the absurd idea. Sleep would no doubt remain elusive all night long. She fished into her apron pocket and pulled out the society page with Mac and Holly's announcement. Smoothing it on the countertop, she stared at the picture.

The happy couple.

Disgusted with her morbid fascination, she tossed the paper into an empty drawer. Why torture herself with thoughts of the Ferguson daughter? Clearly Mac was moving on. He'd come. He'd seen her. He'd made sure that the baby was not his. He'd moved on. Obligation free.

Turning off the hot-plate burner that glowed beneath her teapot, Ella poured the boiling water into her cup and added a tea bag. And—as she stood staring unseeing out the window at the solitary street lamp—she was suddenly transported back nine months to the Brubaker library, that fateful morning after her wedding night.

Ella placed the silver tea tray on the serving table between the two couples in the library. The Fergusons had arrived only moments before, and the four cronies were still in the process of their emotional and somewhat noisy reunion as they all settled into their seats. The four leather wing chairs were arranged in a circle in front of the elegant fireplace, where a fire crackled merrily, warding off the autumn chill. A Beethoven piano concerto tinkled lightly in the background.

Lifting the lid to the silver pot, Ella began to steep the tea, and prepare the condiments for the convenience of the chattering foursome.

"Boy, howdy," Big Daddy thundered, "you two are sure a sight for sore eyes! Trudy, you just keep gettin' prettier every year!"

"Oh, Big Daddy." Trudy giggled, and fluffed her gray-ing curls. Shoulders bobbing with glee, she simpered. "How you do go on."

A secret smile graced Ella's lips as she glanced over at Big Daddy and Miss Clarise. These wonderful people were her in-laws now. Her family. And, their friends would someday be her friends, too. An ebullient feeling of be-longing warmed the cold and hollow corners of her lonely heart. Soon, she would be free to take her rightful place among the family, she mused, as she artfully placed the sugar cubes into a crystal serving dish. Soon the world would know that she was Mrs. Mac Brubaker. She nearly had to bite her tongue to keep from announcing the mar-velous news that bubbled within.

"Well, if you think she's dishy, you oughta get a load of our Holly," George roared proudly, and slapped his knee. Like an overstuffed sofa, his beaming face was but-toned and tufted with dimples. "Now *there's* a sight for sore eyes."

"We were so delighted to hear that Holly has agreed to come out to stay with us this summer," Miss Clarise mur-mured in her cultured Southern drawl. "We are all so look-ing forward to her visit."

"Especially Mac," Big Daddy blustered. "Why I just know that the two of them will hit it off like gangbusters."

Ella's smile faded.

"You know, Big Daddy, I just don't know why the heck we didn't think of it ages ago!" George enthusiastically concurred. "After all, they're from the same basic back-ground." Holding up his meaty hand he began to enumer-ate. "Same education, same social standing, same inborn knowledge of the oil business, same age, same level of drop-dead good-lookin' parents—" his brows waggled teasingly "—and well, doggone it, just about the same everything. I certainly couldn't think of a better match for my precious daughter.''

Heart pounding, Ella gripped the edge of the serving table.

''And I couldn't think of a better match for business, if you get my drift.'' Big Daddy chortled.

''Now, Big Daddy,'' Miss Clarise admonished gently, ''money shouldn't be a consideration when it comes to love.''

''No.'' Big Daddy guffawed, and pointed a stubby finger at George. ''But it sure as heck couldn't hurt. A match like that would set those two kids for life. Hell,'' he shouted, caught up in the moment, ''their great grandkids would be set for life! Pardon my French.'' In deference to the ladies, he doffed his hat.

''All eighty of 'em,'' George crowed.

''Ninety!'' Big Daddy roared.

A rollicking round of laughter filled the room. Ella was grateful for the noise, hoping that it would cover the shattering of her pitiful heart.

They were all hoping that Mac and Holly would marry.

Bertha had been right all along, it would seem. They wanted a wealthy girl from a family of proper social standing and breeding for their son. And could she blame them? Nervously she smoothed her palms over the practical apron of her uniform and closed her eyes against a feeling of doom that settled like a wrecking ball in the pit of her stomach. What had ever possessed her to think that she could fit in here with these people? she wondered, panic causing her head to swim. What had ever possessed her to think that she could marry a Brubaker and actually make a go of it? Looking at it in the harsh light of day, it was ludicrous. She no more fit in here than she would in the royal family. The press alone would crucify her once they caught wind of this story. She could see the headlines now.

The Prince Takes a Pauper.
Gold Digger Snags Her Man.
Wedding Shocker. Oil Magnate Marries Kitchen Help.

Swallowing, she battled back a flood of tears and pasted a bright smile on her lips. Her fairy-tale marriage was going up in smoke. Ella loved Mac too much to saddle him with a marriage that his parents would despise. In the long run, he would only end up resenting her.

With a shaky hand, Ella woodenly began to set the teacups on their saucers.

"I only wish Holly could have come down with you two," Big Daddy confided.

"Yeah, well, she's so caught up in her little charity thing, we're lucky to be able to pry her away for the summer. But, don't worry, old buddy," George assured. "One look at Mac and I will personally guarantee that she will forget those orphans that take up so much of her time."

"Well, I sure hope so," Big Daddy grunted. "And the sooner, the better. The type of girls that Mac has been fraternizing with lately would never do for marriage material. Then again, I've even spotted him hoochie-cooin' it up with some fine members of my staff. Can you believe that? I'm afraid he's gonna chase off one of my best..."

Cups clattered and tea sloshed as Ella fought for her bearings.

"Big Daddy!" Miss Clarise cautioned and daintily ground the tip of her shoe in the toe of his boot.

"What?"

"I was just thinking that perhaps Ella would like to serve the tea now."

"Ella? Oh, yes, Ella! Darlin'! Come over here and pour us a spot of tea, will ya', honey?" To George he boasted, "Ella here is the best little pastry chef this side of France."

"Lucky you, Big Daddy! And so pretty, too. I don't suppose she has a sister?" George teased.

"Oh, George," Trudy giggled. "You leave the Brubaker maid alone now, you hear?"

Smiling, though her heart was breaking, Ella somehow managed to serve the tea and pastries without incident. As the Brubakers and the Fergusons sipped their tea and gobbled up the pile of delicacies she'd placed before them, they continued to congratulate themselves on a match made in heaven.

"No one could ever suit my little Holly, like a Brubaker," George declared, enthusiastically licking the powdered sugar from between his padded fingers.

"Likewise for our Mac," Big Daddy blustered. "Why I can't think of a single girl in the whole world I'd rather have for a daughter-in-law than your little Holly, George! Just think, mutual grandbabies!"

"And mutual stock options," George hollered around a mouthful of petit four.

"And the four of us having an excuse to visit much more often," Trudy added.

"Won't that be nice," Miss Clarise agreed.

After she'd served everyone, Ella sorted out her tray and prepared to head back to the kitchen. If she could find the kitchen. Her head was a swirling mass of misery.

She didn't fit in here.

It was wrong to think she ever could. Wrong. The word reverberated in her brain as she gathered the tray and staggered out of the room. *Wrong, wrong, wrong,* the words echoed over the excited plans of the four friends who sat plotting the lives of their offspring.

Perhaps Stormy had been right after all.

Perhaps it would be better for everyone involved if she simply disappeared off the face of the earth.

A loud pounding on her door startled Ella out of her woolgathering. Lowering her teacup onto the cracked tile drainboard, Ella made her way toward the incessant noise. Clyde must have locked himself out of his small apartment across the hall again, she thought, glad for the company. She didn't really want to be alone tonight, and Clyde's wacky company was better than none.

Pulling the door open, she gasped, discovering much to her surprise that it wasn't Clyde standing in the dingy old hall.

It was Mac.

Not waiting to be invited in, he barged past her, filling the room with his presence. Derision marred his face as he inspected her home.

Clutching the doorknob, Ella quietly closed her door and stared at him through bleary, red-rimmed eyes.

"Nice place," he snorted, taking in the cracked plaster, the dark brown water stains and peeling paint on the walls and ceiling. The only concession to cheer in the dismal dwelling were the brightly colored curtains he'd spotted from the street. As his eyes roved over her room, he noted that with the exception of the small cradle in the corner, the room was set up for one.

Not two. One.

A twin-size wrought-iron bed stood in the corner, its sagging mattress adorned with a threadbare bedspread. A single chrome chair with a tattered plastic seat sat near a Formica-topped table. The burn marks on the top indicated that someone had once used its surface as an ironing board. In lieu of a closet, a bit of dowel had been installed in the corner and the clothes hanging there were dresses. Unless Clyde was a kilt man, Mac suspected he spent little or no time in this room.

"So," he asked, turning to face her, "where's your charming husband?"

Stymied by the question, Ella simply stared at him for a moment.

"You don't know where your husband is? Ella," he teased, "a piece of advice. If you don't keep constant tabs on your spouse, he's likely to get away. Take it from one who knows."

"I thought you'd left town."

"Keeping tabs on me, are you?" He feigned surprise. "I thought you didn't care."

She swallowed and cast her gaze to the floor.

"Well, just so you won't lose any sleep over me, I had a beer over at the Dogleg Tavern and caught up on the local gossip. Then I came back here to borrow your phone directory and make a few phone calls. I'll be happy to reimburse you." His voice was loaded with sarcasm. "I need to make arrangements to spend the night."

"I don't have a phone."

"That figures." Rolling his eyes, Mac shook his head and crossing his arms across his chest, scanned the room. He had a perfectly good cell phone in his Jeep, but he needed an excuse to see her again. "Well, in that case, I guess I simply have to spend the night right here with you and your charming husband. I'm sure he won't mind, once he figures out I'm just your ex-husband and not a government bogeyman." Taking several steps into the room, Mac ran a hand over the rusty wrought iron of the twin bed's headboard. "It's gonna be a tight squeeze, the three of us," he sighed, deliberately goading her. "But that's okay. I'm so tired I could sleep on a barbed-wire fence."

Blushing madly, Ella crossed her arms in a defensive pose over her swollen belly. "Mac, what are you doing here?"

"I might ask you that same question now, might I, Mrs....Johnson, is it?"

"Mac—" her voice quavered uncertainly "—I think it would be much better if you would leave now."

"Because of Clyde's jealousy?" Mac took a step toward her and thoughtfully studied her crimson cheeks. "Well, it might interest you to know that your better half is around the corner at the Dogleg Tavern, yucking it up with the widow Perkins. Why, he didn't even notice me, he was so enthralled with her charms. Hardly seems right, you being so far along in the family way and all." He dropped his gaze to her belly. "Looks to me like you've been pregnant since about...oh, say—" he feigned some mental calculations "—our wedding night?"

"Mac, please, I don't want to have this conversation."

"Why, because you might have to answer a few questions?" he demanded, closing the space between them, and looking her straight in the eye. "Because I might discover the ugly truth? That you never loved me?"

Ella gasped.

Mac struggled to ignore the pain in her expression. No way was she going to thwart his mission, he thought, suddenly distracted by the cool forest green of her eyes. He couldn't get lost in there anymore. He'd worked far too long and hard for this moment, to make a mistake now. He had to know why she left.

"Or, are you afraid that I might discover that your word...your *vow* means nothing?" Reaching out he grabbed her arm and yanked her to him and held her as tightly against his body as the baby in her belly would allow. "That you are incapable of telling the truth?"

"No!" she cried helplessly, and allowed her eyes to drift shut. "You don't understand!"

"What don't I understand, Ella?" he growled. He tilted her head back by tugging on her braid and forcing her to look into his face. "Tell me the truth! I need to know what made you disappear without a trace, the day after I married you, then send me divorce papers the next week!"

"Why this *sudden* need to know?" she taunted, her heated words caressing his chin and lips. "It isn't as if you've spent any time at all pining away after me."

"How do you know what I've been doing since you up and left?" he jeered, his fingers biting into the soft flesh of her upper arm.

Glancing over at her kitchen drawer, she took a breath, as if to answer, then clamped her lips defiantly together. Beneath her bravado, Mac could tell that there was some secret with which she was stubbornly unwilling to part that caused her a great deal of pain. Well, he thought angrily, she may be stubborn, but he wasn't the obstinate Big Daddy's son for nothing. He would simply wait until she came clean. Even if it took the rest of his life. In the meantime, he wanted a few other pertinent answers.

"You can't expect me to believe that the old man busily flirting over a mug of beer is the father of your baby."

She grimaced and remained silent.

"Is the baby mine?"

Ella's eyes narrowed. "The baby is *mine!*" she cried.

"Ella if the baby is mine, I have a right to know! I want to be there for him or her every bit as much as you do."

"Don't make me believe in your fairy tales, Mac," she cried and lifted her imploring gaze to his.

"*Fairy tales?*" he exploded furiously. "What did I ever

do to make you think our relationship was a fairy tale? *You* were the one who left *me,* as I recall!'' Shoving a hand through his hair, he closed his eyes. ''And yet, here I am, like some kind of blasted masochist, trying to find answers that will probably kill me, so that I can get on with my life.''

Ella's throat constricted painfully. ''Mac, I can't do this. When I'm with you, I can't think straight! I never could! That's why I had to leave.''

''*That's* why you had to leave? Because you couldn't *think* straight?''

''No. Yes. No, I... Mac, you have to *go*,'' she cried. ''I know it's hard to understand, but it's for the best.''

''Whose best? Your best? The baby's best?'' he growled, his voice throbbing with unleashed passion and fury. ''Okay, lady, I'll go, but before I do, if *this*,'' he looked derisively around at her shabby room, ''is your idea of thinking *straight*, let me give you something else to think about.''

And with those harsh words, he captured her face between his hands and angling her mouth beneath his, kissed her with all the pent-up passion and loneliness and misery and angst and love that he'd been holding inside for nine long months.

Chapter Six

For a brief moment their lips parted and Ella's knees began to tremble violently. As she gazed into the face that had haunted her dreams for the better part of a year, she blinked back the tears that swam in her eyes. Tears of joy. Tears of fear. Tears of relief.

Her hands lay pinned against his chest, so she twined the fabric of his shirt placket between her fingertips to keep from slipping to the floor. Responding to her unsteadiness, he slipped his arms around her, and the hand that captured her back was as secure as the one that cradled her head.

Again, his head dipped to claim her mouth, this time with a languid sensuality that burst into flame the moment their lips met. Their voracious kiss exploded with a desire far too long denied and, as Mac held her in his arms, a dizzying sense of freedom was released in Ella. Her blood roared in her ears, her heart sang and her breathing came in shallow puffs.

A deep groan welled in Mac's throat at her response.

And, as if he was afraid she might disappear again, just when he'd finally found her, he tightened his embrace.

"Ella," he whispered urgently against her mouth, "I know I'll never forgive myself for admitting this to you, but you have no idea how I've missed you."

"Yes," she breathed, remembering the magic. "I do."

Barely aware of their actions, they automatically fell back into old patterns, responding to the needs that so much time apart had left unfulfilled. Mac took a step forward, drawing her with him and soon had her supported between his body and the uneven surface of the wall.

Lifting his mouth from hers, he nudged her cheek aside and dropped his face into the smooth hollow between her shoulder and neck. As he slowly kissed the warm curve he found there, gooseflesh broke out in a tingling riot along her thighs and upper arms.

Angling her head to give him better access, she pulled him as close as the baby nestled beneath her thrumming heart would allow. One electric inch at a time, his mouth traveled up along her jaw, sending shock waves of delight skittering through her body. Then, as his lips moved to the soft shell of her ear, she could feel him speak her name. The word was strangled. Guttural.

"Ella..." he demanded, "I need to know. Tell me why you left."

Though having him hold her like this was even more poignant than she could have imagined, she knew she had to send him on his way. Taking a stoic breath, she forced herself to whisper, "Because I didn't want to be married...to you. I... I..." she stammered, "I tried to tell you that when you asked me."

"Bull! You can't tell me that you weren't every bit as happy as I was, the last time we were together." His breath teased the wisps of hair at the side of her face as he tightened his embrace.

"I... I..."

"Something happened. Tell me what it was!"

Her mind always left her when he held her this way. "No! Nothing," she gasped.

He kissed her again, then muttered against her lips. "I don't believe you."

A warning bell jangled dully in the back of her passion-fogged mind. This man was engaged to be married. So why was he holding her this way? Because he knew that the best way to render her senseless was to kiss her and caress her and drive all rational thought from her mind. She should push him away. But she couldn't. Not with Mac's hands taking hers and reverently exploring the baby's movements with his fingertips. Against her better judgment, Ella reveled in his touch, loving how nature had taken its course and how her curves had blossomed with motherhood.

With every sweepingly symphonic heartbeat, Ella knew she should stop his fledgling connection with the child. But instead she pressed against his exploring hands, yearning for more, even as she valiantly struggled for her senses.

"We can't do this," she whimpered, her protest muzzy and halfhearted.

"Why not?" Mac whispered, urging her mouth back to his and effectively erasing any rational thought from her brain. He kissed her the way she'd dreamed of for nine long months now. And she was powerless to stop him.

"Because..." she murmured, allowing her head to rest against the cracked plaster of the wall as she tried to remember why they should stay apart. "Because..." Opening her eyes, she pulled back slightly and their gazes tangled. "Oh," she whispered, losing her train of thought once again, "because..."

Mac cupped her cheeks between his palms, and drew his mouth back to hers for more. This time, her mouth was ready. Eager. Bold. They kissed with fiery impatience until Mac—finally remembering why he'd come here in the first place—tore his lips away from hers and released her from his embrace.

Taking a step back, he stared at her through glassy, nearly wild eyes. "It's getting late. I have to go," he said bluntly and plowed unsteady hands through his hair.

"Yes," Ella murmured in a daze, groping for the wall.

Without preamble, Mac strode over to her door, and leaning against it, took a steadying breath. "I'll be back to check on you in the morning." His tone was brusque. Businesslike.

"Where will you be staying?"

"Until I get the answers I'm looking for, I'll find a place to stay here in town." And with that vague hint to his whereabouts, Mac yanked open the door and was gone.

While Ella prepared for bed that evening, she tried to make sense of what had just happened between her and Mac. Emotions battled within as she clutched the iron headboard and gingerly lowered herself to the edge of her bed. Swallowing against the lump that had taken up residence in her throat shortly after Mac's departure, she fished around in her bathrobe pocket and retrieved her hairbrush.

As she brushed her hair, Ella realized that she was more confused now than ever. How could he kiss her that way and be about to marry another woman? Was he in love with Holly, or simply bowing to family pressure? He certainly didn't kiss her as if his affections lay elsewhere.

And what must his fiancée be thinking?

Setting the brush down on the crate that doubled as her nightstand, Ella methodically braided her hair and heaved a sigh that became a sob. She swiped angrily at the tears that were suddenly raining down her face. She was sick of crying. Sick of all the maudlin times she'd given in to self-pity. As a young girl, she'd spent the better part of her childhood secretly crying, hiding her tears. And feeling un-loved and unwanted by the way Stormy begrudgingly al-lowed her to stay with the family, after the death of her father. Unfortunately Ella had had nowhere else to go. After all, she made a handy servant, Stormy would sometimes force herself to concede. Ella was a passable little cook and housekeeper.

She pushed the bitter memories of Stormy to the back of her mind. Ella had made up her mind a long time ago that she was never going to be a burden to anyone again. And that included Mac Brubaker and his blue-blooded fam-ily.

How she desperately missed her father. He would know what to tell her. Sniffing, she rubbed her cheeks with the fuzzy sleeve of her chenille robe.

She wanted so much more for her own child. Not ma-terial things, especially, for she knew of rich people who were vastly unhappy. No, she wanted her son or daughter to grow up knowing that they were loved. And wanted. And cared for. Ella would do anything within her power to make that happen.

The one thing she would not tolerate, however, was Mac's pity. If he was here on some kind of charity rescue mission for her, or the baby, he could take it elsewhere. Even having no father or family other than herself would be better than having her baby grow up knowing that he or she was pitied rather than wanted or loved.

Ella knew about that kind of humiliation, firsthand.

Still, she reminded herself, Mac was not the villain in this scenario. He was as much a victim as she was. It would be natural for him to be curious about her. And the reasons she'd run. And now of course, the baby. She couldn't blame him for wanting answers, but the answers she had to give would only drive a wedge between him and his wonderful family.

She loved him too much to be responsible for such a rift. Family was far too important.

Arranging her pillows to support her back, Ella leaned against the sagging and lumpy mattress and attempted to make herself comfortable. Oh, how her back ached. If only she had a heating pad, or a pair of loving hands to give her a massage. But that was not to be, she thought, the echo of Mac slamming the door behind him still reverberating in her mind.

Shaking her head, she attempted to clear the muddled images of Mac's handsome face that threatened to drive her crazy. But it was impossible. Between the thoughts of Mac and the dull pain that throbbed in her lower back, sleep seemed to be an impossibility. Tucking a pillow alongside her abdomen, she rolled on her side and willed herself to sleep. She knew she needed her rest. For the baby's sake.

She lay perfectly still for a long while, ignoring the pains in her back, and willed herself to relax. Oh, she thought with a sigh as she closed her eyes and ran her fingertips lightly over her lips, his kisses still set her on fire.

Her eyes drifted closed. Sweet thoughts of his arms firmly around her waist, pulling her into the curve of his body, the way they'd slept the night of their wedding, lulled her weary mind. Her body grew heavy as exhaustion took its toll.

She...felt so...secure...just knowing that Mac...was in town... It was...so...wonderful to see him...again. Even if it was...only a...dream.

Ever so slowly, Ella fell into a light slumber where she

and Mac lay entwined in each others' arms, happily anticipating the birth of their baby.

When the old city hall bell tower chimed midnight, Ella woke from her fitful sleep. Something was wrong. Rolling onto her back, she suddenly realized that her robe was damp. Soaked. As was the bedding and her old mattress. Her water had broken. It was time.

As she attempted to sit up, she was suddenly gripped by a pain that took her breath away.

"*Ohhhh,*" she moaned and, doubling over, clutched her belly. "*Ohhhh.*"

When she could breathe again, she reached toward the crate and turned on her bedside lamp. Sure enough, her small alarm clock had reached the stroke of midnight. It would seem, she thought, panting as she waited for the first of her contractions to subside, that she would soon be going from a pumpkin back to a kitchen maid. Soon the worst of it had passed, and Ella scooted to the edge of the bed and began going over her plans.

Clyde. She needed to get Clyde. Then he needed to call the local doctor and have him meet...

"*Ohhhhh,*" she moaned, suddenly doubled over again. This time the pain was slightly more intense. She sat there, her head cradled in her hands, her elbows propped on her knees and waited again for the pain to subside. The baby was coming. She needed to organize her thoughts.

Yes. Okay. Where was she? Oh, yes. Clyde. He needed to call the doctor and then they needed to get on the road to the hospital. It was a twenty-minute drive from Dogleg to Hidden Valley, where the nearest hospital was located.

Breathing hard, she shrugged out of the wet robe. Lifting an afghan off the end of the bed, Ella wrapped it around her light nightie and haltingly worked her way across her apartment. She paused at the door and gritted her teeth through another contraction. They seemed to be coming awfully fast. She would have Clyde time them for her right away. Moving into the hall she shuffled to Clyde's door and knocked. When he didn't answer, she began to pound.

He was gone.

Before she could begin to panic in earnest, another contraction gripped her and bent her in two. Sagging against the wall, she panted, wild-eyed, and wondered what to do next.

Okay, Clyde was gone. Not surprising. Clyde rarely came home before midnight on a Friday night. Trust him to stay out till all hours tonight, she thought churlishly. The night that she was giving birth, no less. Oh, well, how could he have known? She wasn't due for another week, and besides, first babies were notoriously late. She'd given him her blessing to have a night on the town with sweet old Mrs. Perkins. It was his one bright spot in his life since Martha had passed on.

When she could stand upright again, she tried the knob. Locked. And she didn't have a key. And Clyde had the phone. Beads of sweat popped out on her brow as Ella leaned against the cool surface of Clyde's door. Oh, this labor thing was much worse than she'd ever imagined. It made any cramps she'd ever had before mere child's play.

The next contraction hit her hard, and she slid down Clyde's door to land in a crumpled heap of pain on the floor. As she panted her way through the pain, she began to feel nearly delirious.

They were coming too fast.

Perhaps it was because she'd had too much excitement today. Seeing Mac again had put her on edge. Surely if she'd stayed calmer, this wouldn't be happening, she thought, berating herself. Now her baby was in danger. Cries of anguish mingled with her moans.

What was she going to do? She wished she hadn't sent Mac away. Not when she needed him so much right now. After all, he really was the only thing she had that even remotely resembled family.

Suddenly she wished for Miss Clarise's strong, soothing presence. In the two short months she spent with the Brubakers, Miss Clarise was the closest thing to a real mother figure Ella could remember since her own mother's death. Miss Clarise would know what to do.

Why, she'd gone through this hideous process nine times, Ella thought hysterically. It couldn't be that hard. If it was, there wouldn't be so many people on the planet, she reasoned as pain gripped her and carried her away like a runaway freight train. Feeling as if she were being strung up by her abdominal muscles and hung from the ceiling, Ella rode the contraction, and did her best to practice the breathing she'd learned from an old library book.

When the contraction ebbed, Ella clutched her belly and looked back through bleary eyes at the open door to her apartment. It might as well be a million miles away instead of the few steps down the hall that she needed to navigate. With the contractions hitting her so hard and heavy, at this rate, she would never make it to the hospital.

The clock down at city hall was chiming. The deep tones of the bell slowly brought Mac's unconscious mind to the surface. Where was he? he wondered, groggily, and carefully peeled his cheek away from the passenger window of his Jeep. With a shake of his head, he attempted to clear the cobwebs and sit up straight in the vehicle's front seat.

It was midnight.

A vague feeling that something was wrong filled him

with foreboding. Passing a hand over his face, Mac peered across the street to the top floor of Uncle Clyde's Diner. There was a light on in the window of Ella's room. Only an hour ago, it had been dark up there. Yes, something was going on. Did she need his help? He'd parked out here on the street in front of the diner in order to keep an eye on her. Just in case.

He vacillated. What if nothing was wrong? Would it only serve to drive a further wedge between them?

Oh, to heck with the wedge, he thought in disgust.

Finally, unable to stand the suspense, Mac kicked and punched his way out of the down sleeping bag he'd purchased from Barney Jessop's Supply Emporium, and hurled it to the floorboards. Once out of the Jeep, Mac ran across the street and bounded up the back steps that led to Ella's tiny studio apartment.

When he reached the inside of the main hall, he could see that her apartment door was open. Something was definitely wrong. Then, as he made his way toward her door, he heard a low, guttural moan coming from farther down the main hall.

Ella.

And she was lying on the floor in a heap in front of another apartment door.

"Ella?" he rasped, unable to believe his eyes.

"Oh, Mac," she cried in relief as she looked up into his eyes. "I'm…so…*glad*…" she gasped, "…you're here. It's time. The baby's coming."

"The baby's coming?" he repeated dully and, hurrying to her side, knelt down beside her. The truth of the matter hadn't quite sunk into his sleep-fuzzed mind. "What are you doing out here?" he wondered uncertainly, trying to figure out how they should proceed.

Always the powerful businessman, Mac didn't like to

wait around for someone to take charge. He would darn well take charge, even if he didn't know exactly what he was doing.

Fear coiled in his gut as he came fully awake.

"I—" Ella stammered, resting from the last vicious contraction that had nearly rendered her unconscious, "I was looking for...Clyde. He has a phone. *Heeee... Ohhhh... Mac-c-c-c,*" she moaned, closing her eyes and rocking back and forth. "*Ohhhh, Mac. It hurts-s-s-s so bad.*"

"I know, honey, I know," Mac murmured, gathering her into his arms and running a comforting hand over her arm. He didn't know. He didn't have a clue. But whatever was happening, it looked like hell.

"The door is locked...Mac. I have...no way...to call the doctor."

"Who is your doctor?" Mac asked, jumping at this bit of information. The doctor. Now *that,* he could deal with. He stroked the damp tendrils of her hair away from her face.

"Doc Miller." She panted rapidly. "He lives on a ranch...about ten miles from here. *He's-s-s-s*...going to meet me at the hospital when the time comes. Mac." She looked at him, her eyes wide. "The time has come. *Oooooo,*" she moaned. "The time has...*come...now!*" she shrieked, and grasped Mac's hand in a grip that would have given some of his burlier ranch hands a run for their money.

Mac, fearing his own imminent cardiac arrest, decided that they had to have a doctor. Now. Never before in his life had he been so scared. Ella. The baby. They could die.

"Okay, sweetheart, listen. Everything's going to be just fine," he promised, as much for his sake as for hers. "I'm parked out front. I have a phone in my Jeep. We can go to the hospital and call Doc Miller on the way and have him meet us there."

"Nooooo," she moaned. "No. We don't have time to do that. Mac, I'm so scared. The baby is coming! Right now!" Again, her body quaked with the contraction that gripped her. "I have to push, Mac! I have to push now!"

"No!" he shouted. "Don't! Not yet! You can't have this baby yet. Honey, you need help. Help that I don't know how to give you." Frantically he looked up and down the hall, hoping that somehow a team of obstetricians might just happen to be in the neighborhood. At midnight.

Nope, Mac old buddy, he said to himself, you're on your own here. "Anybody else besides Clyde live up here?"

"No. Just..." she panted, "Clyde and me."

"Oh, for criminy sakes... Okay. Listen. I'm going down to the Jeep and get my phone. We can at least call 911. Just hold off on the pushing for another minute, okay, darlin'? I know you can."

"I can't help it, Mac! It's like...like...I *have* to," she whimpered, and proceeded to strain toward expelling the baby into the big wide world. After about a minute of hard work, Ella fell limply back against his lap, her hair and nightgown damp, her eyes at half mast from the exertion.

"Okay. Well, I guess you gotta do what you gotta do," he muttered, holding her tightly in his arms and struggling with his uncooperative brain to form Plan B. Had his own mother gone through this much pain? Eight times? Nine, if he counted Waylon and Willie separately. He was going to have to buy her a new car for mother's day this year.

"I'm so sorry," Ella cried, reaching up and touching his jaw. "I wanted to have my baby in a hospital. With doctors and nurses and a clean bed. Not in the middle of a dirty hallway floor. This," she said with a weak attempt at humor, "is the story of my life." Dismally she looked around, and sniffed. "I'm not due for another week. I can't understand why this is happening."

"Well," Mac said grimly, "whether we understand it or not, it's happening. But not right here, if I have anything to say about it."

With that, he scooped her into his arms and carried her as easily as he had on their wedding night down the hallway and into the room. Setting her on the edge of her bed, he stared at her, suddenly realizing that he might have to deliver this baby himself—a baby he was reasonably sure was his. Jolts of terror mingled with excitement snaked down his spine. Dropping to his knees, he took her face between his hands, and looked into eyes that were dark with agony.

"Ella, sweetheart, do you think you can hang on here for just ten or twenty seconds? I just really need to run down to the Jeep and get the phone..."

"*No!*" she shrieked and began to cry. "*Mac!* Please don't leave me!"

"I'm not leaving, honey, I just need to talk to someone about what we should do here. My experience with birth ends with cattle. Calves are one thing, babies are another. I'll be right back. I promise," he told her with a squeeze of his hand. Before she could protest, he darted out the door, flew down the stairs and tore across the street. Panting with his fear and exertion, he dialed 911.

Quickly explaining his problem, he told the dispatcher Ella's address and the name of her doctor. Then, as he bounded back up the stairs, the cellular phone clutched in his hand, he struggled to absorb some basic advice about the home delivery of babies.

"Centimeters dilated? Uh, I'm not sure. A lot, I guess. A whole bunch!" He shrugged and plunged a hand through his hair as he arrived in Ella's room. "Hell, I don't know. I don't have a slide rule..."

"Mac!" Ella gasped hysterically. "Mac! Hurry! I think I have to push again."

"Hang on!" Mac shouted to both the phone and Ella as he rushed to her side.

Settling next to her as she lay near the edge of the bed, Mac tossed the phone on the floor, where it lay forgotten, as he took in the tortured expression on her face. Wrapping his arms around her, he held her as she rode the crest of another racking contraction. Exhausted, she leaned against him. "Promise you won't leave?"

"I promise. We need to get you under the covers."

"They're soaked," she lamented.

Quickly sizing up the situation on the bed, Mac nudged Ella aside and stripped off the damp bedding. Then, retrieving his cell phone from the floor, consulted 911 for some more advice. Making a mental list, he tossed the phone in the sink and began to scan the room for various tools he might need. Rapidly, he quizzed Ella for their whereabouts.

"Where is your teakettle?"

"On the hot plate," came Ella's listless reply. "It has water in it."

Mac turned it on. "What about fresh bed linens and blankets?"

"There are a few old sheets and blankets in that chest." She gestured to the end of the old iron bed. "They're clean."

"Towels?"

"Same."

"Scissors?"

"Top…kitchen…drawer on the…*lef-f-f-t-t-t-t.*"

"Matches?"

"*S-s-s-same.*"

"Rubbing alcohol?"

"That cabine*t-t-t-t…*over there…by the door." She gritted out the reply through her clenched jaw. The pain was hitting again. Again, Mac rushed to her side and held her hand till it was over.

"Don't leave, Mac," she chanted, sounding nearly delirious from her pain. "Don't…leave."

"I'm right here, honey," he reassured her.

As quickly as humanly possible, Mac made up her bed, and gently assisted her under the covers. When he wasn't helping her breathe through the pain, he was sterilizing pieces of a sheet he'd torn into strips and a pair of scissors he'd found in the cabinet. He was no obstetrician, but perhaps a few of his veterinary skills might come in handy after all. At one point, he broke away to wash his hands with a scrub brush and a dollop of antibacterial soap. Other than that, he didn't know what to do next.

Except to wait.

And take a crash course in child birth from 911.

And pray.

And hope for the best.

Dragging the beat-up old chrome kitchen chair to the edge of the bed, Mac settled in next to Ella and took her hand in his.

"I'm so glad you're here," Ella confessed on a tired sigh. "I don't know what would have happened to me if you hadn't arrived."

"I'm glad I'm here, too," Mac assured her, and dipping a cool cloth into a bowl of water, wrung it out and applied it to the smooth, alabaster skin on her forehead.

"Oh, that feels good," she murmured, and licked her lips. "I'm…so thirsty."

Moving quickly, Mac brought her a glass of water, and held her head as she drank.

"Mmm—" she nodded "—that's better." She lay still for a brief respite, before the contractions took over again. "Mac! I need to push again."

Standing, Mac pulled back the covers and nudged her nightgown aside. Then, with one hand on her thigh, and the other gripping her hand, they went through the contraction together, her body quaking violently with the effort.

Mac glanced at her alarm clock. The pains seemed to be coming about a minute to thirty seconds apart. He didn't know all that much about childbirth, but as far as he could tell, that baby was bent on making its appearance any minute now. He looked with admiration at Ella. She was handling what must be terrible pain with such grace and dignity. The pains ebbed and flowed, each one worse than the last. He looked on in amazement. She was bearing up under the pressure far better than he was.

He only wished there was something he could do to help. To ease the pain.

"Mac," she whispered, "I'm so tired. The…contractions…are coming so fast that I…don't have time to rest."

"I know, sweetheart. I know," Mac murmured and bathed her face with cool water.

"Stop it," she cried, and churlishly pushed at his ministrations. "I'm too cold. And…so…tired."

"I know, honey."

"No, you don't," she shouted deliriously, her head lolling from side to side on her pillow. "You don't know anything about this. You don't know about this baby, or me or how I feel or *anything*," she gasped, growing hysterical. "You don't know what I've been through since I left. I left for your own good, Mac Brubaker. Because it was what your family and their friends wanted. I did it because…it was…all…for the best…for everyone…" she sobbed, "except…me…"

Mac stared at her dumbounded as she ranted. *She'd left*

for the sake of his family and friends? What was she talking about? Was this a key to her motive for leaving? Tucking this information in the back of his mind he decided he would definitely explore it later, when he had a little more time.

"Uh-oh—" she gasped, and reaching for his hand, dug her nails into the soft flesh of his palm "—here we go...*again.*"

Hunching forward on the bed, Ella strained for all she was worth and Mac coached from his position at her side.

"Yes, honey, that's the way," he cried, his voice suddenly excited as he saw the bloody crown of the baby's head. Letting go of her hand, he gripped her knees and settled at the end of the bed. "Come on, baby, breathe," he coached, catching her gaze with his and leading her through this contraction. *"Puuuussshhhh!"* he commanded, and the next thing he knew the baby's tiny head emerged, its wrinkly face puckered into a perplexed frown.

Awestruck, Mac reached out and supported the baby's head, then crowed jubilantly. *"Yes!* So far so good, Ella. The baby's looking good, *great!"* Unbeknownst to him, tears of wonder were streaming down his cheeks. "Amazing," he breathed.

The miracle of childbirth had worked its magic on Mac's shattered heart, healing it to life's smaller problems. Problems that in this heavenly light, hardly seemed to matter anymore.

Exhausted, Ella flopped back on her pillow for a moment. "Are we done?" she moaned, her eyes sliding closed.

"One more push, honey. Just one more and the baby will be here."

"I don't think I have it in me," she murmured.

"I'm...so...tired... Oh, Mac, it...hurts," she stammered, then began to cry.

Mac sympathetically patted her hand. "You're doing a great job, in spite of the pain. Ella, your baby is almost here."

"Here comes another one," she listlessly informed him before she was gripped by one last racking contraction.

"Good girl," Mac praised as she hunched forward and strained until the veins in her neck stood out.

This last contraction brought the baby, kicking and squalling from the quiet safety of Ella's womb. Tiny fists jerking wildly in the air, the baby landed in Mac's large hands.

A son.

Never had Mac felt such incredible awe. Such joy. Such love.

He lifted his eyes to Ella's. "It's—" he choked reverently, suddenly overcome by emotion "—a boy."

And he looked just like every Brubaker son ever born in this great state of Texas. Sparse as it was, his hair was sandy blond, and in typical Brubaker fashion, he sported a pair of deep dimples at the corners of his rosy mouth. And the baby's velvety eyes were the same almond-shaped eyes that stared back at him in the mirror every morning. As Mac looked into these tiny eyes that peered so owlishly up at him, he knew without a doubt that this child was his own flesh and blood. He also knew at that moment, that he would never let this boy out of his life. No matter what.

Excitedly he counted the baby's toes and fingers and wondered what Big Daddy's reaction would be to the news that he had finally gotten his first grandchild. Tucking the phone between his shoulder and ear, Mac crowed his good news to 911 and, grinning like an idiot, dazedly listened to some more instructions on cleaning up the baby.

"A boy?" Ella breathed, and laying back on the pillows, smiled. "A boy." Tears of joy rolled from the corners of her eyes and down her cheeks.

"Yes, and he's all there." Mac laughed as he worked on cleaning the mucous out of the baby's mouth and nose, and swabbing his face and head with a fresh cloth. "And he cleans up rather nicely, too." Quickly tying off the umbilical cord in two places with the strips he'd boiled, Mac took the scissors and severed the lifeline that had held mother to son together for nine long months. "Here," he said, and gently placed the baby on Ella's stomach, "see for yourself."

Peering down into the baby's face, Ella smiled and kissed the tiny cheek. "He is beautiful," she whispered in awe. She looked up at Mac with tears shining in her eyes. "Just like his father."

"Clyde?" He had to ask. Just to make sure.

"No." Ella laughed weakly and rolled her eyes. "You."

When Mac spoke, his voice was gruff with emotion. "What are you thinking about naming him?"

Reaching down, Ella stroked the baby's sticky curls with a loving fingertip. "I think…Garth."

"Garth?" Mac asked, puzzled.

"For your father."

"Big Daddy?"

"Mmm-hmm. I know how he likes Garth Brooks, and figured we may as well carry on the family tradition. Garth Brubaker has a nice ring, don't you think?"

"Ella Brubaker…"

"Hmm?"

"I sure do love you."

"I know," she said with a wan smile. "That's part of the problem."

Chapter Seven

An hour later, after having finished up where Mac left off, Doc Miller packed up his black medical bag and beamingly pronounced Ella and Garth both fit as fiddles.

"Nice job, for a G-man, son," the old gent chuckled, clapping Mac heartily on the back. "If you ever get tired of the spy game, you have a real talent for medicine." At Mac's puzzled expression, the jovial doctor laughed till his face glowed red. Pointing to Ella, he winked and instructed, "Ask your wife to fill you in on the local gossip."

"Yeah, I heard some of it earlier tonight, down at the tavern." Mac shrugged good-naturedly.

"Small town," Doc Miller said and grinned. "Oh, and Mac…" Pausing at the table, he scribbled out a prescription with a thoughtful frown. "I'd like you to bring these two into the clinic tomorrow, so that I can see how things are progressing. For now, though, I want them to stay put and get some rest." Tearing the prescription off the pad, he handed it to Mac. "You have my number, in case you should need anything between now and then." Reaching out, he shook Mac's hand. "Congratulations on a beautiful son, you two."

"Thank you." Mac smiled broadly.

Shrugging into his light overcoat, Doc Miller popped his bowler onto his snow-white head and quirked a scolding brow at Ella. "Don't hesitate to call, you hear? And this time," he teased, "don't wait until the last minute."

Ella's smile was tired. "No problem."

"We've got the phone right here," Mac assured him, gesturing to his cell phone. He opened the door for him, and proceeded to walk Doc Miller back to his car.

Ella and the baby were alone when she heard a familiar voice at the door.

"Babe?"

"Come on in, Clyde," Ella called from the bed where she lay with her newborn son.

Poking his head through the door, Clyde stared at her in shock for a moment and then pointed a shaky finger at the baby. "Where'd ya get him?" he asked, wonder and amazement showing clearly in his wrinkled face.

"He showed up about an hour or so ago," she explained with a tender smile. "Come on in and meet my son. This is Garth."

"Garth?" Hobbling across the room, Clyde moved to the chair next to the bed and peered at the cherub that lay in her arms. His grizzly features softened.

"How do you like him?" Ella asked, proudly pulling the cloth away to better display her son's angelic face.

"Oh," the old man breathed with reverence. His eyes were suspiciously bright. "He's a keeper, Babe."

"Yes," Ella murmured, determination in the soft word. She would keep him. Somehow.

Slowly Clyde lowered his aging frame into the chrome chair and leaned toward her. Disappointment flashed in his expression. "I saw Doc Miller's car out front and came a runnin' up the stairs as fast as my old leg would allow just now. I'm truly sorry I wasn't here fer ya when ya needed me. I really meant to be, it's just that I didn't know—"

"Clyde, please." Ella interrupted him with a shake of her head. "Please, don't worry about that. You've always been here for me when I've needed you the most. I can never repay you for everything that you've done for me."

Her throat closing at the poignant look on his face, Ella grasped his knobby, age-spotted hand and squeezed to show him that she meant these words with all her heart. She loved Clyde. The way she imagined a daughter would love a caring father. Then, releasing his hand, she reached out and stroked the old man's leathery cheek with the back of her finger. It was damp from the tears that had sprung unbidden to his pale blue eyes.

"Would you like to hold him?" she asked gently.

"Could I?" he whispered, and held out his bony arms to receive the tiny bundle. "Oh, my goodness," he said, his gravelly voice halting. He blinked rapidly down at the baby nestled against his sunken chest. "My Martha always wanted one of these so bad. We just never…I don't know." Bending over, he pressed his lips to the baby's forehead.

"I'm sorry."

Clyde shrugged. "Don't be." With a shake of his head, he threw off his maudlin memories, and smiled a wide, gap-toothed smile at her. "The diner was always my baby. But I gotta tell ya, it's not nearly as cuddly as this little guy."

For a moment he *tsked* and cooed and whispered some gibberish that Garth seemed to understand, then the old duffer peered up at Ella.

"So," Clyde's grin faded and his brow furrowed into a wiry line of curiosity as he softly patted the baby's back, "how'd you manage to have him, up here all alone?"

"She had some help."

The masculine voice at the door had Clyde's head jerking around. Recognizing Mac—as he observed from the doorway, his arms folded across his chest—Clyde's mouth dropped.

"Luckily Mac was here to help me when I went into labor," Ella explained, sending a thankful look at Mac.

"He was?" Clyde asked stupefied, his expression clearly wondering where this new turn of events put him in the federal tax scheme.

"Mmm-hmm. Actually Mac delivered the baby," she told him, more than a tinge of pride in her voice.

"He *did?*"

"Yes," Ella said, her lips tipped at the corners at his bewildered expression. "Clyde—" she gestured at Mac "—this is Mac Brubaker. Garth's father." Might as well let everyone know. It was no secret anymore.

"He *is?*" Craning his neck, Clyde's jaw dropped as he stared at Mac. "The baby's father is a G-man?"

Sighing, Mac pushed off the door casing and ambled across the room to the bed. He sunk to the edge of the mattress next to Ella, and ran a hand over his unshaven jaw. "Would someone mind filling me in on how this G-man business got started?"

Ella's smile was amused. "Mac, tell Clyde that you're not here to arrest him for tax fraud."

"Tax fraud?" Mac frowned at Clyde. "Whatever gave you that idea?"

"Oh, nuthin'. Just a little…you know…creative accountin' on my part." Sheepishly Clyde lifted and dropped a bony shoulder. "So you're not a G-man. Well, hot doggy. In that case, it's nice to know ya." A low cackle rumbled deep in his chest. "And just so ya don't beat me up in a jealous rage or nuthin', you should probably know that Babe here ain't my wife,'' he joshed.

"So I've gathered," Mac said dryly.

"You here to take Babe back to wherever you come from?" Clyde asked, looking suddenly crestfallen. He held Garth a little more tightly to his chest.

"No," Ella hastened to assure him, even as the question broke her heart. "Mac has his own life now, and I have mine." She darted a quick glimpse at Mac, and noted that his face had grown suddenly stony.

"Good. Good. That's nice." Clyde nodded at Mac, then, with a grunt of effort, Clyde passed the baby to Ella. "Here ya go, Babe. It's plumb past my bedtime. Uncle Clyde had a big night tonight, wooin' Mrs. Perkins." The old man's laughter wheezed out like sandpaper roughing up a chalkboard. He cocked a minxish grin as he slowly unfolded his body from the chair. Then, giving Ella a tender kiss on the forehead, he slowly shuffled to the door. Before he disappeared into the hall, he turned and waved. "Don't be a stranger now, Brubaker."

"I don't plan on it," Mac said grimly. His voice held a promise.

It was nearly dawn by the time Mac managed to get Garth settled in, the room cleaned, the bedding changed again, and crawl in next to Ella. After moving the bed up against the wall, Mac stripped down to his shorts, then wedged his aching body between the cracked plaster and Ella. The bed was lumpy and cramped, but Mac couldn't have cared less. It was a place to rest his weary bones, and better yet, it held the woman he'd discovered—once more—that he loved.

Yes. He knew it was true. He'd never stopped loving Ella. Never would. No matter what.

Too tired to worry about what the future held for them, Mac gently gathered Ella in his arms and cuddled her against his body, the way he'd been dreaming of since the day after he took her to be his wife. The baby was nestled in the cradle over on Ella's side of the bed, and together the three of them drifted off into a peaceful sleep, a family at last.

The small, lamblike cry of his tiny son brought Mac to the surface of his slumber. Sunlight was beginning to filter into the room, casting a diffusing glow across the harsh reality of their surroundings. It was so warm and comfortable pressed between the cushion of blankets against the wall and Ella's soft back. So secure. The tiny lamb continued to bleat, and Mac smiled languidly in the twilight before he came fully awake. More than any other place on earth, Mac was exactly where he wanted to be. Right here, resting peacefully with his wife and son.

Still wrapped in his arms, Ella stirred. The baby's cry grew lusty, and Mac could feel her coming awake as well.

"I'll get him," Mac volunteered, whispering sleepily into her hair.

"Mmm." Stretching, Ella shook her head and smiled. "Don't bother." Reaching up she pushed a lock of Mac's hair away from his eyes, and then trailing lower, allowed her hand to linger for a moment against his stubbled jaw. "Unfortunately I don't think you have what he wants."

The look on her face was soft and loving and it filled Mac's heart with a dull ache of desire for uncomplicated days gone by. Clasping her hand between his cheek and shoulder, he kissed and nibbled her fingertips.

"Ah. Perhaps you're right," Mac agreed as he watched her roll away from him and lift the baby out of the cradle. Laying on her side, she tucked the baby against her stomach and brought his tiny, rosebud mouth to her breast. Immediately, little Garth's crying stopped, as he enthusiastically worked on his breakfast.

"He seems pretty healthy," Mac murmured, the pride in his voice unmistakable. Leaning over her shoulder, he admired his little boy, already so robust and sturdy. A love, like none he'd ever known before was blooming in his heart. No wonder Big Daddy was always interfering with his children's lives. He could understand now, how it felt to want the very best for your child.

"Mmm-hmm," Ella agreed, gently smiling down at the tiny mouth and cheeks that instinctively suckled. "He has dimples. Deep ones. Just like you." The pad of her finger traced the dent in the incredibly soft cheek.

"We all have 'em." Mac chuckled, amazed at the many similarities between his son, and the rest of the Brubaker clan. "They'll work well for him later in life, when it comes to attracting girls."

Ella huffed and feigned indignation. "So you think that's why I fell for you? For your dimples?"

"Well, it was either that, or my soulful brown eyes."

Rolling her own eyes, Ella bit back a smile. "Don't you listen to him, Garth," she whispered to the baby. "You're going to grow up and be a gentleman aren't you?"

"I'm a gentleman," Mac argued, defending himself.

"Yes, you are." Stilling, Ella tucked her chin to her shoulder and looked back at him. "I don't know what I would have done without you, last night."

Their gazes caught and flashed with the wonder of this new bond between them.

"For a while there, I was beginning to wonder if I was going to be much help to you."

"You were perfect."

"Well, the timing was, anyway." He lifted a shoulder.

"Almost as if it was meant to be, me waking up and finding you before he arrived."

"Mmm." Ella nodded, and felt a peace steal into her soul. Being here with Mac felt so right. It was becoming easier with each passing moment to forget the problems with their marriage. To forget about Holly. To imagine that everything would eventually work out fine, and that could continue to exist in this little microcosm of time. Easy, but unrealistic.

"How are you feeling this morning?" Mac asked. He gave the back of her thigh a gentle pat. After what he'd seen her go through last night, he was surprised she had the strength to have this conversation, let alone nurse their son.

"Everything hurts. My face, my eyes, my neck...even my hair hurts," she moaned, and settled more firmly against his body.

"That bad?" Mac murmured sympathetically.

"I feel like I've been run over by a steamroller. But," she amended with a chuckle, "in a good way."

Mac laughed. "In a good way?"

"Mmm-hmm. If that's what it takes to end up with this little guy, then I'm all for it."

"I bet you wouldn't have said that last night."

"Probably not." Ella smiled.

Together they turned and gazed in adoration at their son—whose thirst having finally been slaked, had drifted off to sleep—as his small cheek pillowed against Ella's breast.

"You did well, Ella. He's beautiful." Mac's voice was thick with emotion.

"Well, I didn't do it all by myself," she murmured, leaning back and glancing up at him.

"I seem to remember."

Their gazes clung and held for a long, loaded moment—
a moment loaded with wonderful, thrilling memories, as
well as memories of betrayal and pain. And, of course, with
a multitude of unanswered questions on both parts. Questions that neither of them seemed ready nor strong enough
to delve into at this point in time. As if by silent, mutual
agreement, they were enjoying whatever precious little time
they had left together in a denial of sorts, where they could
pretend, at least, to be a real family.

Languidly Ella allowed her mind to flirt with the idea
that this could actually happen.

"Are you hungry?" Mac asked, whispering now, to keep
from waking Garth.

"Mmm. Famished."

"Me, too. But then," he murmured, running his hand
over her hip, "we had a pretty wild night last night."

"I know I worked up an appetite." Ella smiled softly.
"Why don't you go on downstairs and get Clyde to rustle
us up something to eat?"

"What time is it?"

Ella peered over at her alarm clock. "Six."

"Aw, man," Mac groaned. "We only slept for a couple
of hours."

"Well," she said, giving him an impatient nudge, "go
get us some breakfast, and when we're done eating we can
take a nap."

Leaning forward, Mac growled into her neck. "You
know, you really got this nagging wife routine down pat
since I've seen you last," he teased.

"Just go get the food," she ordered, the twinkle in her
eyes belying the stern sound of her words.

"Yes, ma'am. Will Clyde be up already?"

"Mmm-hmm. The diner opens at seven for breakfast."

"Okay then, I'll be back soon with food." He sat up

and, catching her delicate chin with his thumb and finger, forced her to look into his eyes. "You're not going anywhere?" he asked, only half teasing.

"No," she whispered solemnly, realizing the vulnerability that hovered beneath the surface of his smile. "I promise. I'll be here when you get back."

"I won't be long."

"Good." Already she was growing dependent on his wonderful presence.

Scooting to the end of the bed, Mac—as carefully as possible—climbed over Ella's legs, then stood and reached for his pants.

Ella's thoughts couldn't help but harken back to their wedding night, as she watched him tug his faded jeans up over his lean hips. Deftly his fingers worked the buttons up to his navel, and her eyes continued the trail across his flat stomach, and up across his broad pectorals. He was such a beautiful man. Pride of an ownership she knew didn't really exist, filled her heart. No wonder she'd fallen under his spell those many months ago. He was irresistible.

Snagging his shirt off the iron footboard of the bed, he lifted it over his head, found the sleeves and let it float into place on his body. Ella swallowed.

Unaware of her train of thought, Mac smiled at her—a blatantly sexy smile that lifted his upper lip and brought out the dimples that were identical to his tiny son's. Slowly he winked at her as he tugged his collar into place, then fastened the buttons on his shirt placket.

She struggled to remain detached, but it was too late. Hope had begun to blossom. Mac was back. Did she dare believe he would stay? Could she regain his trust? The bed creaked with his weight as he sat down and reached for his boots.

Uncertainty plagued her as she watched him work his

feet into the well-worn leather, then stand and move toward the door. Perhaps while he was here, she could try to make him happy. If, by some twist of fate, he broke off his engagement to Holly and stayed in Dogleg, she would know for certain that Mac understood the stark reality to which he was committing himself this time. This time, unlike the whirlwind fairy tale they'd plunged into so many months ago, Mac would be walking into this life with his eyes open.

"So, is it true what Ella said last night? That you don't want her in your new life?" Clyde squinted at Mac as he whipped the pancake batter in his bowl to a smooth consistency.

"Clyde," Mac sighed and paused for a moment. Cocking a hip against the baking table, he folded his arms across his chest and pondered the old man's words. "I honestly don't know where she got that idea."

Clyde shrugged. "Yeah, well, women are funny creatures. Just when ya think ya have 'em figured out..." Clicking the inside of his cheek, he stared intently at Mac.

From the moment he'd stepped into the kitchen that morning, Clyde had pelted Mac with questions. Before Mac knew it, he'd shared a good deal of his life story with the diner's owner, up to and including the part where he met and married Ella. It was obvious how much the older man had come to care for Ella in these past few months. And, because of his respect for their relationship, Mac found himself answering questions aloud that he hadn't even asked himself.

"So, you *do* want her back?"

"Yes."

"Because of the baby?"

"Yes and no."

That answer seemed to satisfy Clyde immensely. "You still really love her, don'tcha, boy?"

"More than I ever thought it possible to love another human being." Mac took a deep breath and scratched the stubble on his jaw. "In spite of everything."

"In spite of everything," Clyde parroted and tossed a handful of fresh blueberries into the bowl. "What everything?" His face wadded into a wrinkled mishmash of curiosity as he leaned toward Mac and slowly folded the berries into the batter with a rubber spatula.

"Ella never told you what happened between us?"

"Hell, boy," Clyde snorted, "she never even told me her name was Ella. Not that I didn't try to worm it out of her." Lips stretched into a wide smile, he revealed the many gaps in his teeth.

"She didn't tell you she was married?"

"Nope. But I figured there was a man in her life somewhere, her bein' in the family way, and all."

"So, I guess that must mean she didn't tell you why she ran away."

"No. Why'd she run away?" Clyde stopped stirring, fascinated.

"Beats the hell out of me." Mac kneaded the tense muscles at the back of his neck.

"She don't seem like the type to run away. She never run away from me," the old geezer mused.

Mac rolled his eyes. "Well, obviously, she had some reason for leaving. And I'm here to find out what it was," he said vehemently. "She's been here with you for quite a while now, Clyde. Can you think of anything she said over the past months that may give us a clue?"

Clyde put down his bowl, and rested his elbows on the baking table. Grinding his fists into his baggy, bloodshot eyes, he forced the rusty wheels of his memory into motion.

"Well, she never did say nothin' specific about you, if that's what you're gettin' at," he began and trained his translucent blue gaze on Mac. "But I do know that she's been sad for a real long time. Sometimes she'd like to gaze out the window, just a thinkin' away. When she thought I wasn't lookin', she let a tear or two fall. Once I asked her if she wanted me to try and get in touch with the father of the child, thinkin' that might make her feel better. But, no, she said the father of her child was far better off without the likes of her. I couldn't hardly believe that." Clyde arched an accusing brow. "I can't imagine that you'd tell that little gal such a thing, now wouldja?"

"No!"

Clyde grinned. "Jest checkin'. Well, anyhow, the only thing she'd say on the matter was that she didn't fit in with his kin. That's all. When I tried to dig a little deeper, she'd always distract me some way or another."

Didn't fit in with his kin? What the devil did that mean? Was that the reason she'd run? Mac frowned and added this to what she'd muttered so deliriously last night about leaving him for the sake of his family. But that hardly seemed likely. The Brubakers had never treated members of the staff like second-class citizens. Big Daddy had always gone out of his way to make sure that his kids treated everyone with respect, regardless of their station in life. Had something happened to make Ella believe that his family wouldn't accept her?

Clyde moved to the cooler and pulled out a slab of bacon and a carton of eggs. As the old man scraped and oiled the grill, Mac puzzled over his dilemma. Soon, the woodsy smell of frying bacon began to fill the air.

It was clear that for whatever reason, Ella felt that she couldn't live in his world. So, he thought as a plan began to germinate in the back of his mind, perhaps he would simply have to live in hers.

"Clyde?"

"Yeah, hmm?" With machinelike precision, the old man formed a row of perfectly round, perfectly sized pancakes.

"You know of any property for sale around here?"

Clyde snorted and poked at the sizzling bacon with a fork. "You kiddin'? Everything's for sale 'round these parts. "Folks can't *give* their land away since our one and only oil field up and blew away. Heck," he cackled dryly, "for the right price I might be talked into sellin' my baby. Why do you ask?"

Lifting a thoughtful shoulder, Mac stared out the order window and into the dusty, vacant street. "I was just thinking. If Ella doesn't want to live with me, maybe I ought to come live with her."

With his spatula, Clyde expertly lifted the edge of a pancake and peered underneath. "Mighty noble of ya. Life's too short not to take a chance now and again." Arching a pliant brow, he seemed to mull that pearl of wisdom over himself before he spoke again. "So," he asked, casting his line into the conversational pond, "know anything about runnin' a diner?"

"Why?"

"Ella likes it here."

"What's your point?"

"I've been thinkin' of retirin' and makin' an honest woman out of the widow Perkins. I ain't gettin' any younger, ya know. Besides, she's always yacking about honeymooning at Disney World." After he'd turned the bacon, he began cracking eggs.

"Disney World?"

"She's a big kid at heart." Clyde's raspy cackle rattled around the kitchen.

"Then that would make you two perfect for each other," Mac said, and laughed.

"Just like you and Ella."

Mac sobered. The old man had a very good point. Life was far too short to let another precious second escape without Ella. And Garth, he thought fiercely, a wellspring of love for them both flowing in his heart.

"But Disney World and—" Clyde pulled a sly frown as he stroked his silver stubbled chin "—the Bahamas, now that takes some money."

Snagging an order pad and a pencil from the chrome countertop, Mac scribbled a number and slid it over into Clyde's view.

Clyde swallowed, his jaw sagging. "Oh, yeah. Now *that* might just cover it."

Mac grinned.

Suddenly the older man's saggy, basset hound face wore a tender expression. "You promise to take good care of them two, now, you hear? That girl—she's—" he choked, and blinked "—she's real special."

"Yes." Mac nodded, his throat thick with emotion.

"And—" his watery eyes traveled slowly around the dilapidated kitchen "—you'll be good to my baby?"

"Count on it."

"Good enough." Clyde's lower lip quivered even as he smiled.

Mac grasped the old man's blue veined hand for a handshake to seal their deal, but Clyde—having other ideas— wouldn't let him get away that easily. Pulling Mac into his scrawny embrace, the old man pounded him on the back. "Good luck, Brubaker."

"Thanks," Mac said. "I think I'm going to need it."

"Closed? Gone fishing?"

Her brow furrowed, Ella stared in surprise at the makeshift sign Clyde had hung in the window of the diner. For as long as Ella had known him, Clyde had never even so much as gone across the street without telling her what for and how long he expected to be gone.

After parking the Jeep next to the curb in front of the diner, Mac tugged on the emergency brake and unfastened his seat belt. They were just now returning from their appointment at the clinic with Doc Miller. Garth, strapped securely into the little car seat that Mac had recently purchased at a shop in town, snoozed peacefully in the back seat.

"What could that mean?" she wondered aloud. "Clyde never goes fishing. He doesn't even like fish."

"He mentioned something about needing a vacation this morning when he was fixing us breakfast," Mac said with a grin. He pointed to the handmade banner under the Gone Fishing sign. It's A Boy! scrawled in Clyde's shaky penmanship proclaimed the good news to the curious townfolk. "Since you don't need him anymore, he decided to take a little time for himself."

Of course. How selfish of her. Ella nibbled the inside of her cheek between her teeth. He was getting on in years. It was natural that she would worry. Oh well. Clyde had a right to his own life. She would get by until he returned.

Mac was still here. Just the thought caused her heart to flutter.

"It's about time he took a vacation," Ella murmured. "He works far too hard for a man his age."

"How old is he?" Mac asked.

"He'll be eighty-six on his next birthday."

"*Eight-six?*"

"Mmm-hmm," Ella said and smiled at his shocked expression. "I was surprised when he told me, too."

"Well, I'll be a son of a gun." Mac shook his head and stared thoughtfully out the windshield. "I hope I'm half as spry as he is when I'm his age."

Ella's chuckle was strained. "Today, I think I *am* his age." It was true. Just getting up the stairs and into her apartment was a daunting thought. Thank God for Mac.

Mac turned to look at her sympathetically. "We need to get you back into bed."

Again, her heart thumped erratically at his words. Words that evoked images of a sweeter time.

"Yes," she murmured, her gaze locking with his. "That would be nice."

Chapter Eight

"**W**hat's this?" Shuffling slowly behind Mac as they entered her apartment, Ella stopped and stared: Standing there in front of her in all its shiny new glory, was a brand-new double bed. Brass. With a new comforter and pillow shams. Slowly her eyes traveled over to the corner, where a glider rocker sat, waiting to send the baby to the land of nod.

"Just a little birthday present for Garth," Mac told her with a broad grin that told her how pleased he was with himself. Moving over to the kitchen area, he set the baby— still in his car seat—down on the tabletop. "And, I have to admit, it's kind of a present for me, too. No offense, Ella, but my poor back couldn't take another night in that rickety old bed."

Ella cast her gaze back at the gleaming bed that looked as if it had been plucked straight out of the department store's showroom window. She couldn't look at Mac.

Was he really planning to stay? Had he had time to give

thought to his career with Brubaker International? His family?

Pulling her lower lip between her teeth, she stared at the cheerful flowers on the chintz pillow shams and matching dust ruffle, in a daze.

He hadn't spoken of the future yet. He hadn't mentioned his engagement to Holly, nor had he had the time to call and break it off with her. Or to inform his family that he was leaving the company for that matter.

Perhaps he was not leaving Holly. Or the company.

Perhaps he simply hated her old bed.

Tears of confusion filled her eyes.

The new bed was already assembled and made up with new linens. The old bed had miraculously disappeared. These were the kinds of things that Mac had the money to do. She had to admit that he could give their son things she could never dream of.

Except—she thought fiercely and dabbed her eyes with the back of her sleeve—for a mother's love. Only *she* could give that to Garth. Holly could never love their son the way she did.

"Mac, I can't let you do this."

Turning, she brought her gaze to his hopeful, boyish face and her heart melted. She had to give him an out. She had to let him know that she and the baby would survive, if he chose Holly. She had to be strong. But it was hard, especially when she was so vulnerable. As it was, her hormones were screaming at her to beg him to stay. But she couldn't do that. His powerful family had great expectations for him. A life here in Dogleg certainly was not on their agenda.

"This—" she gestured weakly to the bed and then to the rocker "—it's too much."

Mac mistook the tears in her eyes for those of joy.

"No," he assured her, shaking his head as he strode over

to the rocker and sat down to demonstrate the smooth ride.
"It's not too much. Look, Ella, it fits right here in this
corner just perfectly. We're going to love it. Garth," he
said with fatherly pride, "is the one who's going to love
it." He looked up at her, his face shining with expectancy.
"I had to take a chance on the color and everything, but if
you don't like it, we can always exchange it for another
one. The guy I talked to on the phone says this one is their
most popular model."

"You can't stay," she suddenly heard herself blurt out.
The words sounded much harsher than she'd meant them.
She simply wanted him to know that he was free to go, if
he chose. *Please don't go*, she silently pleaded. *Please
choose us.*

The hopeful light in his eyes faded and his expression
grew hard.

"I— I—" she stammered, and needing to sit down,
moved to the chrome chair at the table. Oh, dear. She was
fumbling this badly. And her energy, both emotional and
physical, was flagging. Gingerly she lowered her sore and
aching body to the uncomfortable little chair. "I know you
will, um, have to go back to...your—" she couldn't force
Holly's name past her lips "—job, sooner or later." The
murmured words were barely audible.

"You can't get rid of me that easily, Ella," he growled,
his voice low. Then, seeing her angst, he ran a hand over
his face in an effort to erase his frustration and pull himself
together.

"But, Mac," Ella whispered, her heart in her throat, "I
know..."

"Listen," he commanded, holding up a hand to forestall
any more conversation in this direction. "Let's not talk
about the future right now. Or the past, for that matter.
We've just had a baby. Let's...just enjoy our son. We can

sort this whole mess out later. In a few days. When you're feeling stronger."

Too tired to argue, Ella studied his face for a moment and could see that he meant business. Her longing gaze strayed to the bed, and seemingly of their own volition, her legs brought her to a standing position, then shuffled her over to the bed. Probing the mattress with her fingertips, Ella could no longer resist the call of comfort. She kicked off her shoes, pulled back the covers and slid beneath the crisp, cool sheets. It felt heavenly. She was so incredibly tired.

"Why don't you rest for a while?" Mac needlessly suggested. "I can take care of him." He motioned to the table where Little Garth was still sound asleep from the car ride home.

"Mmm," Ella agreed. Slowly her eyes drifted shut, her head cradled against the downy softness of her new pillow. As she lay there, sleep flirting with her mind, her bruised and battered body began to relax. Sleep. So tempting. "Yes," she murmured, already dreaming. She would rest, but just for a little while.

Ella was not sure how much time had passed when her eyelids slowly began to flutter open. Through the heavy fringe of her lashes, she could see Mac over in the corner, tenderly rocking his son, and singing silly little cowboy songs in a clear, soothing voice. He was smiling into the baby's tiny face with such a sweet expression of love, that Ella feared her heart would stop beating from the extreme poignancy of it all.

Mac's large hands cradled the baby's soft, fuzzy head, and Garth was contentedly sucking on his father's pinkie. The low tones of Mac's conversation was fraught with cooing and sweet nothings as he rocked and murmured and became acquainted with his new son.

"Well now," he said, referring to his little finger, "it's certainly not mama, but then, there's nothing like our mama, huh, buddy?"

Garth blinked inquisitively up at his dad.

"Yep." Mac nodded sagely.

To Ella, Mac somehow resembled—in ways that transcended physical appearance—Big Daddy. She smiled at his loving, paternal streak. If he turned out just like Big Daddy, he would make a fine father, someday.

"Oh, yeah," Mac continued. "I know how you feel. I still feel the same way about my own mama. Miss Clarise. She's a special lady. You're gonna love having her for your grandma. No doubt she'll spoil you rotten." Mac's dimples slowly came out of hiding.

As he continued to rock the baby and tell him stories about his youth, and how Big Daddy would be so happy to hear about him, and how he met Ella and how he fell in love with her, Ella felt the tears swim in her eyes. Tears of happiness. Of sorrow. Of love.

"...and you will never have to worry because you will always know that your daddy sure loves you and your mommy." Lifting the baby from his lap to his chest, Mac pressed his lips against the tiny forehead.

Ella lay still, her fists bunching the hem of the sheet to her cheeks as she listened. Confusion chipped away at the resolve she'd spent nine long months constructing in her mind. From the way Mac was bonding so tightly with his son, she was beginning to see that she would be wrong to interfere with their relationship.

A slow smile worked its way to her lips. He was so good with the baby. A natural-born father. She always thought—from the moment they met—that he would make a wonderful dad for some lucky child. Fiercely protective, understanding, loving, caring and generous to a fault. Those were the reasons she'd married him. And those were the reasons she'd left.

Burrowing under the covers, she watched father and son with a contented heart. This is the way it should be, between parents and children. The way Mac tickled Garth under his chin, and kissed the top of his tiny bald head made her long for her own sweet father. He would have been very proud of his grandson. His untimely death had robbed him of these precious moments. But, Big Daddy was still alive. And Miss Clarise. They deserved to know about Garth. For a long moment, Ella mulled these thoughts over in her mind.

"You're gettin' pretty hungry, huh, partner," Mac mused as little Garth screwed up his face and looked about ready to cry. "Me, too."

Garth squeaked uncomfortably.

"You know," he told the baby as he shifted him up to his shoulder and began to pat his small back, "your uncle Clyde left me the keys to the kitchen this morning when he left. Says there's lots of stuff to cook down there. Too bad all I know how to cook is pancakes. And I learned that from watching Uncle Clyde this morning. That's okay. I know how to make some kinds of sandwiches, too. And chips. I know how to make those. Just open the bag. I'll show you how, later, when you have some teeth. When your mama wakes up, I'll go rustle us up some grub, okay?"

"I'm awake," Ella murmured. Brushing her hair back from her face, she propped herself up on her elbow, her hand cradling her head as she regarded her little family.

"Well, hi there, Mommy," Mac said, and sent her a gentle smile. "You've been asleep for quite a while now."

"Mmm, thank you for letting me rest."

At the sound of his mother's voice, Garth began to cry.

"No problem," Mac said, jogging the baby up and down and patting his back. "I think he might be hungry. I know he's dry, because I just changed him."

"You did?" Ella smiled at the mental picture.

"Yep. We figured it out all by ourselves, right, pardner?"

Garth shrieked lustily, knowing Ella's voice meant supper.

"If you feed him," Mac volunteered as he scooted out of the rocker and moved over to the bed, "I'll feed us."

"That sounds like a really good deal."

With great care, Mac handed his precious son over to Ella. After a quick kiss on both their cheeks, Mac strode to the door.

"And Mac?"

Pausing, he turned and looked softly at her. "Hmm?"

"Thanks." For the third time since they'd arrived home that day, she felt her eyes brim with tears. What an emotional idiot she was being. Crying because he was making her a silly sandwich. Crying because she couldn't do it for herself. "I—" she sniffed and smiled tremulously up at him, as she realized the sad truth of her words "—couldn't have made it without you."

"I know how you feel. I've been there—" his gaze was penetrating as he studied her tearstained face "—recently myself."

The days seemed to pass like lightning, and before Ella knew it, Mac had been in town for the better part of a week. And, even though Ella was feeling better, stronger and more like her old self, they were still operating under Mac's directive that they not discuss the future or the past. Nevertheless, it weighed heavily on both their minds. However, they managed to carry on in this little bubble of happiness, finding joy in simply being together, and discovering the wonders of parenting a baby.

Since Mac was especially partial to bathtime with Garth, in the mornings, Ella would set up the small plastic tub in the kitchen sink, and on the counter she would gather the necessities such as towels and soap. Then, she would stand back and watch the suds fly as man and child happily figured out the basics of bathing and being bathed.

"Whoa there, little buddy," Mac crowed as Garth escaped his firm grasp. "You're gettin' kinda slippery." His sleeves were rolled up to the elbow, and he wore one of Clyde's old aprons tied around his waist.

"Here," Ella suggested, "use this." She handed him a washcloth.

"Thanks, Mommy nurse." Mac grinned at the baby. "Isn't Mommy nurse pretty?"

Garth burbled some nonsense in answer.

"Yep." Mac nodded. "I think so, too. Very yummy. I thought so from the moment I laid eyes on her."

Angling his head, he sent her a scorchingly sexy look that caused a hot pink flush to crawl up her neck and settle in her cheeks.

"Mac!"

"What?" He arched an innocent brow.

"Not in front of the baby," she mumbled, for lack of a better response.

Mac threw back his head and laughed. "Hear that, squirt? If I want to flirt with your mama, I'm going to have to put you to bed."

Garth stared at his father, his lips curving, his arms jerking excitedly.

"Hey, Ella," Mac whispered in awe, "look! He's smiling!"

Eyes wide, Ella peered at her son, and knew a maternal

pride so strong it stole her breath. "You know," she said, catching the coattails of Mac's enthusiasm and going along for the ride, "I think you're right! They always say that it's just gas, when they're this young. But I don't believe it. He's really smiling at you." She tilted her head to look at Mac's proud to bursting profile.

"Yeah, he's smiling all right. But I think it's at you."

"No." Ella shook her head, loving the way his body brushed against hers as he soaped and lathered the baby. "You spend just as much time with him as I do. I think he prefers you."

Even as he shook his head in denial, Mac beamed at her sweet words. "You know, I think he's going to have your nose."

Leaning against Mac's powerful arm, Ella pretended to study her son's nose. More for the opportunity to touch Mac than any other reason. "When I look at him, I see a miniature version of Big Daddy."

Hooting, Mac nudged her with his elbow. "Only because of all this wispy stuff sticking out of the top of his bald head. That," he said, chuckling, "and the fact that he doesn't have far to go before he's Big Daddy's height."

"Oh, you're terrible." Ella giggled.

Propping himself on his elbows against the edge of the sink, Mac tucked his chin into his shoulder, and quirked a playful brow at her. "You have some soapsuds on your cheek," he told her, his gaze roving over her face.

Impulsively Ella arched forward and brushed her cheek against his shoulder.

"Didn't get 'em. Here, I can help you with that." Scooping a handful of bubbles from the water, he touched them to her nose and cheeks then laughed at her long-suffering expression.

"Mac."

"Here, I think I know a way to get rid of all those bubbles." Propping Garth on his little foam pillow, Mac took his hands away from his son and framed them at Ella's face, his thumbs smoothing her cheeks and brushing over her nose. "That's better," he murmured, then before he could change his mind, settled his lips over hers for a slow, sweet, languid, heart-stopping kiss. "Mmm," he whispered against her cheek, "I've been wanting to do that all morning."

"Me, too," Ella admitted and looked deeply into his eyes for a long moment, studying the changes that this last year had wrought. He looked older now, with new tiny lines of worry etched at the corners of his eyes and mouth. Lines that she had no doubt caused.

The baby's birth seemed to have brought even more changes in Mac. In him, she could see a deeper, more fierce sense of commitment than ever before. A maturity of sorts, that left behind the carefree cowboy who had wooed her and talked her into eloping nearly a year ago. Parenthood was changing Mac. If possible, for the better.

At the same time, Ella could see how parenthood was changing her. Having this child made her lie awake at night, rethinking her relationship with Mac. Ella knew that she must think of what was best for the baby. Not, particularly, what was best for the parents. Perhaps, she thought, pondering this dilemma as she studied Mac's sweet, familiar features, this meant giving her child the father he deserved, regardless of their future as a couple. In her wildest dreams, she couldn't imagine anyone but Mac filling that role.

She stared up at Mac's incredibly handsome face, a woman torn. It would be so lovely to have a continuing relationship with Mac.

But at the same time, Ella knew herself. She could never

share him with another woman. It would eventually tear her heart out to stand by and watch him remarry and give Garth a bunch of stepsiblings.

How on earth did Holly figure into this wacky family portrait? she wondered in irritation. For a couple engaged to be married, they certainly didn't put a high priority on communication.

Mac pulled her close for another heart-stopping kiss, and Ella knew this was not the touch of a man in love with his fiancée. Besides, Mac was far too honorable to string her along this way. Wasn't he?

Garth gurgled and splashed, bringing them back to the present. Ending their kiss, Mac had to let go of her and steady himself against the countertop.

"Ella," he sighed with a teasing grin, "let's run away and get married."

Ella felt a smile bloom, in spite of herself. "Been there," she whispered coyly, and touched a fingertip to his lips, "done that."

"What is this?"

"Casserole."

Ella's nose wrinkled as she looked across her kitchen table at Mac. He was seated in the chrome chair, she in the rocker. Little Garth was fast asleep in the cradle. "What's in it?"

"I don't know. A little of everything."

"It's not SuperDog dog chow, is it? I know how you like that stuff." She laughed till her face turned red.

Mac huffed and sent her a martyred glance. "You know where the kitchen is." He pointed dramatically at the floor where Clyde's diner lay quietly waiting to reopen for business. "If you think you can do better, go for it."

"Of course I can do better," she said, giggling and goading him. "I'm a cook."

"Oh, yeah right. Rub it in," he complained and feigned a wound in the vicinity of his heart. "Okay, tomorrow, you get cooking duty. I can take care of my little pardner while you rustle us up some fancified grub." His elaborate cowboy drawl had her laughing.

"*Ohhhh, no!* You're not getting out of your cooking duties that easily," she declared. Tentatively she dipped her spoon into Mac's so-called stew and took a taste. "What's in it?"

"Noodles. And tuna. And cheese."

"Go on."

"And bacon bits and catsup and taco mix. Oh, and some soy sauce. And a potato chip crust."

"You're sure those black chunks aren't SuperDog?"

He snorted.

"Okay," she conceded, making a wry face as she tossed her spoon on the table. "You don't have to cook anymore."

"Thanks a lot," Mac muttered, secretly pleased. He hated his cooking, too.

"It's okay," she told him. "I think it's time for me to get back to work." A crease of worry marred her brow. "If Clyde ever decides to show up again, that is. He's been gone for a week." Bringing her large, slightly concerned gaze to Mac she set down her spoon and studied him. "You're sure Clyde didn't say anything about when he was going to return?"

"No, in fact he was pretty vague about that." Mac ducked his head. If he sustained eye contact with her, she would know he was up to something.

"Well, I'm starting to get worried. In the first place, Clyde never claimed to like fish that much. Wouldn't even serve it in the diner. And he never, I mean never, stays away from his 'baby' for more than a day at a time. In fact, from what I gather, I don't think he took a day off since he and Martha bought the place.''

Mac shrugged noncommittally.

Ella continued. ''Except for the day of her funeral,'' she amended, ''but even then, Clyde claimed she'd want him to keep the place open and carry on.'' Arching across the table, Ella narrowed a confidential look at Mac. ''Although, I don't really believe that she'd want him to work as hard as he has all these years. I like to believe that Martha would want him to slow down some. Smell the coffee. You know what I mean?''

Rocking his head slowly up and down, Mac nodded. ''Yes. I know what you mean. Sometimes, escaping the rat race can be just what the doctor ordered,'' he agreed contentedly. Ignoring his casserole, Mac buttered a piece of toast he'd managed not to burn.

''Well, anyway, I'm beginning to worry.''

''Clyde's a big boy. I'm sure wherever he is, he's having a great time.''

Mac concentrated on his toast, feeling a little guilty about not telling her the whole story. Oh well. He had the feeling their little heart-to-heart would be coming sooner than later. Yes, the time was growing nigh, to get down to brass tacks. Soon enough she would discover he'd purchased the diner. And soon enough, he would discover her reaction to that purchase. A seedling of uneasiness took root in his confidence. Shrugging it off, he changed his train of thought.

''Give me this,'' he ordered, pulling her still-full bowl of casserole out from under her nose, ''I can make you a sandwich, if you're still hungry.''

She grinned. ''No, thanks. I had a bowl of cereal while you were downstairs cooking.''

"You cheater." Pouting, Mac stacked their dishes and carried them to the sink.

"Oh," Ella sighed, "now don't go and get all sulky on me."

"I can sulk if I darn well please." He bit back a smile as she came up behind him and, slipping her arms around his waist, peered up into his face. "I slave away all day over the hot stove, and what do you do? You're up here dining sumptuously on corn flakes."

"I wouldn't exactly call it sumptuous," Ella said with a laugh, the mirth bubbling into her throat and tinkling past her lips. Pushing her head under his arm, she ducked between him and the countertop.

"It's okay," he sniffed and blinked theatrically as he reached around her and set their casserole in the sink. "I know you're only trying to be nice."

Ella gripped his waist, her smiling face swaying, mere inches from his own. "Yes, I am. And you aren't being very cooperative."

"Oh…so it's…*cooperation* that you want," he growled and wrapped her in his arms. "Now that I can do," he murmured into her hair, his voice thick.

Mac heard Ella suck in a breath. He closed his eyes in the echo of that breath and ran his hands up her back. Removing the clip to her braid, he set her long locks free and filled his hands with her wavy mane. Her body felt so good against his.

He'd been waiting for so long.

And, though he knew it would be another long while before they could come together as man and wife again, Mac couldn't step back. He wanted Ella. More with every passing second they spent together. In the wake of the hollowness that had haunted his heart over the last year, holding Ella this way was such a relief.

"Oh, Mac." His name passed her lips on little more than a sigh.

He gathered her more tightly into his embrace, fear and worry about the direction of the future driving him as he covered her cheeks and neck with possessive kisses, and then proceeded to devour her mouth. His head swam from the torment this confusion caused.

They had to talk.

Soon.

It was just a matter of finding the right time.

And this—Mac thought as he slowly lifted his lips from hers and tried to bring his breathing under control—was definitely not the right time.

"We...uh—" he cleared his throat "—need to do these dishes before Garth wakes up."

As if on cue Garth began to squeak in his sleep.

"I guess you're elected to clean up," Ella said saucily, and kissed him on the nose. "But don't worry," she teased as she lifted the fussing baby from his bed, "we'll stay here and supervise."

"Lucky me," Mac murmured, and meant it. A restless feeling filled his gut as he watched Ella settle into the rocking chair with the baby. The sweet sound of her lullaby quietly filled the hushed room. Unbuttoning her blouse, she drew the baby close for his evening meal, and Mac suddenly felt about as close to paradise as any human on earth could feel.

With the small exception of their future.

Sighing, he turned to fill the sink with hot soapy water and stared out the dusty paned window. The sun had already sunk beyond the horizon. It was amazing how quickly the days had flown by since he'd been here in Dogleg. Already it was getting late. Another day, lost forever. He glanced at his son's tiny face. The sands of time were slipping through his grasp, and he was powerless to stop them. Suddenly he knew more than ever why his parents not only had so many children, but tried to keep them all so close.

Unfortunately Mac was learning it was impossible to control another's destiny.

Finishing up the dishes, Mac tossed the damp dish towel over his shoulder and turned to lean a hip against the counter. Ella had finished nursing Garth and was now changing him and getting him ready to go down for the night. She was so beautiful to watch, going through these simple tasks, smiling gently and humming softly.

A feeling of desperation clawed at his belly. What was she going to say when she discovered that he bought the diner from Clyde? Would she feel trapped again? Threaten to leave?

Well, if she did, it was just too darn bad, he thought grimly. He was as serious as a heart attack about never letting her go again. No matter what her reasons were for leaving him in the first place, they could conquer them. It was one of the things he'd promised her when he proposed.

With her by his side, he could conquer the world. And he would, even if he had to follow her to the ends of the damn thing to do it.

A last pat on his round belly, taut with his meal, and Garth was down for the count. Slowly straightening, Ella stretched and probed the small of her back, and smiled with loving tenderness at her son.

"Ready for bed?" she whispered, glancing up at Mac from where he stood against the counter, observing them, lost in thought.

"Oh. Um. Yes," Mac sighed and slipped the damp dish towel over the refrigerator's door handle.

Yes, he was ready. More than she'd ever know.

Chapter Nine

"**Y**ou awake?" Mac whispered lightly into the gloaming.

Turning on her side, Ella faced him. "Yes," she whispered back. Their hushed words and Garth's light breathing were the only sounds inside the predawn room. Outside, a few morning birds twittered, hailing the arrival of the first rays of sun.

"I thought so." His gaze traversed her face, and came to rest where the shining mass of her hair melded into the pillowcase. Disentangling his arm from under the covers he reached out to stroke a golden lock of hair away from her face and let his fingers trail down to her smooth, bare shoulder. "What are you doing awake already? You need your rest." Lightly he toyed with a tendril of her hair as they lay nose to nose, smiling at each other.

Ella shrugged then burrowed farther under the covers, and studied him with a blissful expression in her eyes. "I couldn't sleep."

"Why not?"

"I was just thinking."

"What about?"

"Um." She lifted a shoulder, wondering how deeply she should reveal her thoughts and fears. Soon now, they were going to have to discuss the issues. They couldn't put it off forever. For the moment, however, she decided to tread lightly. "You. About how sweet you've been, to you know, stay here and rough it with us for so long now."

"What roughing it?" Mac stretched languidly, and yawned. "This is a brand-new bed, woman. I may never leave."

She could feel her smile grow melancholy. Would that it were so. His legs brushed against hers, in a way that was familiar and wonderful. She wished she could wake up just this way, every morning for the rest of her life.

"You know what I mean." She gestured to the dark brown water stains in the ceiling and to the missing chunks of plaster below the window. "This isn't exactly the Ritz."

"Yeah, well—" he puffed his chest and arched a rakish brow "—I've got roughing it in the blood."

Ella snorted in a most unladylike way and nudged Mac with the palm of her hand. "Get out of here," she guffawed, then covered her mouth so as not to wake the baby. "You call having a team of maids and cooks and chauffeurs at your every beck and call, roughing it?"

"No." Mac shook his head, seemingly unfazed by her rather cynical view of his life out at the ranch. "You oughta go on a cattle drive with us someday, if you think I don't know how to get my hands dirty. Sometimes we leave the motor home at the house and everything." Smiling, his expression slowly became somber and he looked at her for a long, piercing moment. "Actually when I say I have it in my blood, I was referring to my father."

"Big Daddy?"

"Mmm-hmm. It may surprise you to know that he wasn't born with a silver spoon in his mouth. Our family is made up of many things, but old money is not one of them. Big Daddy was born dirt poor to two parents who, on some occasions, could serve up only a batch of love for dinner to him and his brothers and sisters. To this day Big Daddy still wonders how they managed to get by on what his father was able to make at the factory where he worked. They didn't have much, but Big Daddy always knew he was loved. And that's been my father's credo his whole life. Family. Love. And the love of your family."

Ella stared at Mac for a long while, reconciling this new version of her husband's family in her mind. No wonder she felt such an immediate kinship with Big Daddy. It seemed they had a lot in common.

Until, of course, the point in her life where her father died and any love she may have harbored for family had been worked or beaten out of her by Stormy. She had a healthy respect now for the opinions of "family" members. They could ruin your life, if they were so inclined.

There, it seemed, her background parted ways with that of Mac's father. And Mac as well. They were worlds apart.

Was it time she realized and accepted once and for all, that there could never be a real future for her and Mac? She sighed heavily. Even Bertha had made that clear from the beginning.

Clutching the sheets to her chest, Ella pushed herself to a sitting position and leaned against the brass headboard. The sun, now peeking over the horizon, was beginning to filter into the room through the grimy panes of glass that made up her front window. She stared morosely out into the street, suddenly realizing the time had finally come.

Again.

Time to move away from this fantasyland, and get on with real life.

It had been well over a week now, and for whatever reason, Mac had not allowed any serious references to the future. She couldn't continue to live in limbo this way. If he didn't want to commit, she wouldn't blame him after what she'd put him through, but still, she had to get on with her life.

She finally had to accept that expecting Mac to stay was nothing but a pipe dream. If he intended to stay, he'd have said so by now. A lump the size of an orange lodged in her throat.

Somewhere outside, a rooster emitted a strangled shout, signaling the beginning of a new day and symbolizing the beginning of a new life for Ella. It was time. She was feeling better now, at least physically speaking. Mac would eventually have to return to his old life at the ranch. His career at Brubaker International. Holly.

For the sake of her poor bruised and battered heart, if he was going to leave, sooner would most decidedly be better than later. The longer he stayed, the more desperately she wanted him to. For Garth. For herself.

She had to say something to him. Now.

"So, you see," Mac said in an irreverent tone as he smothered a yawn, "I hail from hearty stock. Living here in Dogleg hasn't been that awful."

Ella froze, sure he didn't mean to insult her. Taking a deep breath, she smiled brightly at him.

"Well, your childhood was a little different than Big Daddy's was. Or mine, for that matter. And because of that, you now have choices. Options." Unable to help herself, her tone was brittle. Fragile as glass. "Responsibilities."

Mac paused and stared at her for a moment. As if he

suddenly realized that she was about to burst their happy little bubble world, he lifted a sardonic brow.

"Oh?" The word was hard as his eyes scanned her suddenly stiff demeanor. Grabbing the pillows behind him, he plumped them almost viciously and pulled himself to a sitting position next to her. He then sat quietly, studying his hands as they lay in his lap. Only the muscle that jerked in his neck gave any indication to his feelings as he listened to Ella speak.

As generously as she could—given the fact that her heart was breaking—Ella began the much overdue process of sending Mac on his way. With a cool grace that would have made the Queen Mother proud, Ella gazed benignly over at him and vowed that not a tear would fall today. She wouldn't crack. She'd had almost two weeks now to rehearse this moment in her mind.

Why then, was it so blessed hard to say what needed to be said?

She took a deep, steadying breath.

"You, of course, need to be getting back, I'm sure. You have a company to run and—" she choked and cleared her throat "—other obligations. I...I'm feeling fine and strong now. Surely, Clyde will be back very soon and he will need help down in the kitchen."

Peeking at his stony expression, she waited for his response. He could say something, she thought churlishly. Anything. He could argue. Call her a fool. But he didn't. No. He simply stared at her.

She took a deep, irritated breath. "You can't stay, so that's...that. Right?" With all her heart she wished he'd shout, *Wrong! I can stay. I'm breaking off my engagement.* But things never had a habit of working out that way for Ella.

Unable to bear the lengthening silence that roared between them, Ella fumbled for her robe and slipped it on over her shoulders. Sliding her feet out from under the covers, she gave her sash an efficient yank, then padded over to check on the baby. Garth was peacefully sleeping, blessedly oblivious to the drama being played out by his parents. Ignoring Mac, Ella purposefully moved over to the sink and began preparing their morning cup of coffee.

Mac watched and with all that was within him, bit back his anger at her cavalier words. With jerky movements, she flipped on the hot plate, then found a filter in the cupboard. Pot rattling, she shoved it under the faucet and let the water flow full blast.

Mac narrowed his eyes at her back. How the devil could she possibly still think that he was simply going to pack his bags and go skipping out of their lives and into the sunset? Hadn't he put in his time here? Hadn't he convinced her that he wanted to stay in this godforsaken town with her? Hadn't he shown her how much he loved her? The baby? Hadn't he shown her how much he was willing to forget and forgive?

With each question, his blood boiled hotter.

"If you think you're sending me away, you'd better sit down and do some serious rethinking." Mac's voice was low with fury, the words forced out between his tightly clenched jaw. Roughly tossing off the comforter, he jumped out of bed and, reaching for the pile on the floor, began jerking on his clothes. His voice was harsh with anger as he spoke.

"We have it all now, Ella," he growled, hiking his jeans up over his hips and buttoning them with lightning fingers. "And you want to throw it all away. I can't understand you! Okay. Let's have it out now. You owe me the truth. I'm not leaving until you tell me why you ran! And even then, dammit,'' he jeered, pointing an accusatory finger at her, ''I'm not *leaving!*''

Ella stopped measuring the coffee grounds and slowly turned to face him, her face ashen. ''You can't keep that promise,'' she whispered.

''What the hell are you talking about? Dammit, Ella! Tell me. I want to know. I need to know. *Now.*'' He took a step toward her, his body radiating with an anger that was nearly palpable in its intensity.

''You want to know?'' she asked, her lower lip trembling, her knees shaking violently. ''Okay. You should know.''

Woodenly she opened the drawer near her hip and, reaching into the back, fumbled around till she pulled out his engagement announcement. She passed it to him with a jittery hand.

Mac stared at the paper she'd handed him, his mouth agog.

''What?'' he whispered as his eyes moved over the printed words. *''What...on...earth?''* With a shake of his head, he jerked his gaze from the engagement announcement to her face. ''I had nothing to do with this.'' Savagely he pointed at his picture. ''I didn't even know it was in the paper. This picture was taken at a family barbecue last month. Big Daddy must have sent this in.''

''Then, you admit, you are going to marry Holly,'' she stated dully.

''No!''

Ella closed her eyes, knowing he couldn't be telling her the truth. Perhaps to spare her feelings. Well, she was a big girl. She could take it. In spite of the fact that her heart was bleeding to death.

Seeing her skeptical expression, he attempted to explain. ''Yes, we were engaged.''

Her battered heart sank with a thud.

"But, it's not what you think. I can explain that." He moved toward her, his hands outstretched.

"Oh, sure." She couldn't keep the hurt from her voice. "Go ahead and explain how you could find yourself engaged, just months after marrying me." Deliberately she turned her back on him and continued preparing the coffee.

Mac snorted and dropped his arms. "I told you I have a perfectly good explanation, but first, *I* deserve an explanation. *I* want you to tell me why *you* ran." Crossing the room, he grabbed the coffeepot out of her hands and forced her to look into his face. "This—" he held the announcement to her nose "—doesn't tell me anything."

Never had Ella seen him so angry. She glanced over at the still peacefully sleeping baby. Thankfully Garth was a heavy sleeper. She couldn't bear for him to wake while they were fighting.

"Keep your voice down," she beseeched, feeling tired and older than Clyde. "I don't want to scare the baby."

"Then why don't you have a seat," he suggested, his tone low with fury as he shoved the chrome chair over at her and pointed, "and tell me all about it."

Clasping her robe at her throat, Ella gratefully did as she was bid, considering her knees had turned to the consistency of a half-cooked pudding. Once settled, she pushed her hair away from her flushed cheeks, and grimacing, crept back in her mind through the pain and hurt, to the morning she'd decided to leave Mac.

"Your...parents," she began haltingly, and ran her tongue over her dry lips, "were having a tea for their guests, the Fergusons." She glanced up at him to see his reaction. He didn't flinch. "The morning after our wedding night."

"Go on," he directed, his words clipped as he leaned

against the counter, his arms folded in a defensive posture across his broad chest.

"They..." She swallowed and blinked at the hot tears that scalded the backs of her eyes. "They were all so happy to see each other. It seemed that the reason they'd gotten together was to plan the time when their daughter, Holly—" she motioned to Holly's smiling face as it peeked out at them from the paper he held "—would come out for a visit."

A muscle twitched at the corner of Mac's mouth.

Reaching into her pocket, Ella pulled out a tissue and began to twist it between her fingers. "She was coming...it, uh, seemed, to meet you. To...spend the summer with...you." She hated the way her voice sounded so tinny and high. It felt as if a helium-filled balloon had lodged in her voice box.

"Yes." Mac nodded impatiently.

She continued haltingly. "They were all so happy that you were both...single. That...you would both get together again after all these years and no doubt fall...in—" she shuddered as the incomprehensible thought ran up her back "—love."

A low, masculine grunt of disgust emanated from deep within Mac.

"I was shocked, of course, being that I was already your wife." She lifted her liquid gaze to his steely eyes. "But I knew that they couldn't know that. In a way, I was glad that you'd decided not to tell them yet. But in another way, I wanted to scream at them and tell them that I was your wife and to beg them to stop talking. But, they didn't." A lone tear forced its way down her blotchy cheek.

"Th-they were all so, ah, happy that they were going to be related. After all these years, the idea was so exciting to them. They were like kids at Christmas. They—" she paused and blew her nose "—talked about everything that you two have in common."

Mac groaned and glanced around as if looking for something to hit.

"No, Mac, don't. Listen. They were right. They said you came from the same background. That you had the same education. That you came from the same social circle, and that you even had the same knowledge of the family business. Oil. Money. Big business. They said..." She laughed a hollow, bitter laugh. "They said that they just couldn't envision a better match for their son."

Plowing a hand through his hair, Mac listened in shocked disbelief.

"But to top it all off," Ella continued brokenly, "they said they were worried about you getting too chummy with certain members of the kitchen staff." She waved an airy hand, her smile lopsided, her eyes bleary at the memory. "Then, your mother realized I was in the room and hushed them up."

A sound that was part sob, part laughter squeaked past her lips. Closing her eyes, she divested her soul of the last painful part of this scene.

"Oh and the best part was, as a consolation prize of sorts for the poor embarrassed kitchen girl that you'd been so erroneously flirting with, they all admired the way I poured the tea." Mimicking their blustery Southern drawl, Ella brokenly repeated George's words.

"Why, you're a lucky son of a gun, Brubaker! Does she have a sister? I could use one like her in my kitchen. Then Mrs. Ferguson laughed and told him to stop teasing the—" her lips quivered as she faltered "—servant."

Heaving a long, slow sigh, as if her heart were too heavy to beat, Ella brought her tearful gaze to Mac. "I didn't fit in, Mac. I knew then and there that I never would. Not ever."

"What?" he asked, completely dumbfounded. *"That's* the reason you left? Because you overheard my father picking out my wife?" He shook his head in disbelief. "You don't give me any credit for knowing what *I* want? Who *I* deem qualified to be my wife? You don't trust me," he flung at her, hurt and agony etched in his eyes.

"No, Mac," Ella cried. "And there's the proof." She gestured to the newspaper that still dangled between his fingertips.

"This? Oh, Ella," he groaned, suddenly exhausted, "it's not what it looks like."

"Then what is it, Mac?" she asked, a plaintive note in her quiet voice.

"It's *nothing!* You ran off and took our baby with you, all for nothing!" He fairly vibrated with impotent rage.

Going rigid, Ella shook her head. "Mac, I didn't know I was pregnant when I left. I figured it was better to simply cut our losses while we both still had a chance."

"But you didn't come back after you discovered you *were* pregnant." Mac hurled the bitter words at her.

"Don't you see?" Ella cried, frustrated with his obtuse view of the situation. "As much as I want to believe, to pretend, I realized that I could never fit in! I'm not like…Holly. A baby and I would have just been a noose around your neck. Eventually you would have grown to resent us for holding you back from the things Big Daddy has planned for your life."

"I plan my own life!" he spat, keeping his rage low, so as not to wake his innocently sleeping son.

Losing steam, Ella tiredly passed her hands across her face and pushed her hair back over her shoulder. "If it makes you feel any better, I thought about calling you, just before the baby was born, but when I saw the engagement announcement, I knew I'd made the right decision.''

"The *right* decision? How do you know it was *the right damn decision?* You didn't even give me a chance to discuss it. You just took it upon yourself to save the world. To save my family from a pastry chef for a daughter-in-law. To save me from a life with the woman I love. To save me from the son I didn't even know I had!''

Fit to be tied, Mac reached behind him and turned the water faucet on full blast and dunked his head. He was way beyond counting to ten. Grabbing a towel from a drawer, he buried his face in it, and leaned on the counter, his back to Ella.

"Ella..." he sighed, exhaling heavily and closing his eyes for a moment. "I think I understand why you thought doing what you did might help, but you have to understand what you did to me by leaving. I know you've been through hell, since you left. But, dammit, so have I!'' He pounded his fist on the drain board for emphasis, and little Garth stirred in his sleep.

"Mac," Ella began tentatively, knowing that he was at the end of his rope, and not knowing what that might mean, "I heard your family. I heard the Fergusons. They would never accept me.''

Oh, what a hideous mess this was turning out to be. She should have gotten lost, and stayed lost. Stormy's harsh laughter taunted the recesses of her mind.

"Mac, you are engaged now. I've grown to accept that. But I cannot and will not live where I have to have my nose rubbed in it all the time. I—I—" she blinked rapidly as she stared at his back "—have limits, too," she told him, the tears now flowing down her crumpled features. "Holly is a better choice in the long run.''

Mac blanched. Dragging the towel away from his face,

he turned to face her. The engagement to Holly was not real. But, how could she know that? Would she believe him, even if he told her? He could only try.

"Ella," he sighed, wondering how he could ever make her believe, "Listen to me. I was never really engaged to Holly."

Accusation sparkled in her eyes. "Spare me, Mac," she said dispassionately. "There it is, in black-and-white. I know what I saw in the paper."

He stared at his and Holly's phony engagement picture, his heart sinking with the sudden realization that the hole he'd dug just may be too deep to crawl out of. The thought that they lost precious months together because she'd overheard Big Daddy scheming about getting him married off to Holly, seared his heart like a knife.

Furious at Ella for being so gullible, furious at Big Daddy for being so interfering, furious at himself for being such an idiot, Mac didn't trust himself to speak.

He'd been robbed.

Robbed of his honeymoon.

Robbed of his wife's pregnancy.

Robbed of being able to shout his love for Ella McCloskey from the rooftops.

He needed air.

Striding to the door, he yanked it open and looked her straight in the eye. "Obviously nothing I have to say will change your mind about me," he said, his voice deadly calm, now that he knew the score. Now that he knew that his worst enemy was himself.

Mac Brubaker hadn't gotten to the top of the heap in the business world without knowing how to handle a crisis or two.

Sustaining their magnetic eye contact, Mac knew without a mist of a doubt, that he was wildly in love with the woman who was gazing so tragically at him from across the beat-up old kitchen table.

He had also come to the epiphany that same moment, that none of this would have happened if he'd handled things properly in the first place. If he'd told the truth. If he'd announced to the world, his intentions to take Ella as his wife, his family would have embraced her with open arms, and they'd be back at the ranch this very moment, proudly showing Big Daddy and Miss Clarise their very first grandson. But, thanks to his idiocy, here they were, living in a falling-down, one-room flat in the middle of Dogleg, Texas, the very future of their relationship on the line.

As their gazes tangled in a sad, pathetic slow dance, Mac knew he was going to have to find some way to prove his love to her. He knew he needed to take an action of some kind that would convince her that there was no way he could live without her love. Talking was all fine and dandy, but Ella needed to be shown.

"I gotta go," he muttered, eager to put the plan that was formulating in the back of his mind into action. Without a backward glance, Mac headed into the hallway, slamming the door behind him.

Garth began to cry.

Ella stared after Mac, dumbfounded. "Mac!" she cried. "No! Wait!" But it was too late.

She'd finally convinced him to leave.

Unfortunately she realized that's not what she wanted at all.

Slumping forward across the tabletop, she buried her head in her hands and cried as her heart broke once more.

Chapter Ten

Finally, by midmorning, Ella had managed to stop crying. She'd had to. Garth had needed her attention. Seeing her red face scrunched up and flowing with tears the way it had been all morning, had him screaming like a banshee. The poor little munchkin. He didn't understand what was happening.

Ella settled with him in the rocker that Mac had bought, and tried to convince Garth—or herself, she couldn't be sure which—that they would be just fine without daddy. For hours they rocked, Ella's head in a murky bog of emotion, and Garth, sensing his mother's angst, fussed the morning away.

And so, the morning came and went.

And then, the afternoon.

Obviously, she thought dispiritedly, slogging through the hours in a deepening depression, Mac had finally come to the conclusion that they were better off without each other.

Well…good.

She sniffed and dabbed her eyes with Garth's receiving

blanket. That was what she'd been angling for him to realize all this time, wasn't it? Why then did she feel as if the earth had suddenly stopped rotating? Every nerve ending was on alert in her body. Hoping against hope, she mentally strained toward the front door and wished with all her being that at any minute, Mac would walk through that door to stay. For good. They would laugh, and hug and cry and promise never to fight again. He would tell her that he didn't love Holly. Never did.

However, as one minute ticked away after another, the entire day managed to pass through the hourglass without a word from Mac.

When the dusky fingers of night came creeping into the room that evening, Ella went through the rituals of bathing, nursing, changing and singing to Garth, by rote. Other than that, the only thing she'd managed to accomplish that entire evening was a quick shower and shampoo for herself. Even that was a tremendous effort, given her frame of mind.

Forgoing dinner due to a lack of appetite and willingness to prepare anything, Ella slipped into her nightgown and fumbled with the buttons at her throat. Teeth chattering, lips trembling, hands shaky and faltering, her body fairly vibrated with remorse. With regret. She'd made a terrible mistake once again, it would seem. She should have told Mac how she felt about him. About how much she loved and wanted him. About how she needed him to be there for their son.

But it was too late.

He was gone.

She looked into the drowsy eyes of the babe that lay in the cradle next to her bed. Would this child ever forgive her for robbing him of his father? Shoulders drooping with the monumental responsibilities that she was sure she hadn't even begun to imagine, Ella shuffled closer to her son.

Once she'd tucked the baby into his little bed and turned out the light, she stood in the dim moonlight as it filtered in through the window. Finger-combing her still damp locks, she stared hollowly at the bed she'd shared with Mac for the past two weeks.

It looked so incredibly empty. Her heart thudded limply beneath her breast and tears pooled in the corners of her eyes. Lifting the comforter, still crackling with newness, Ella slipped beneath its cool surface, and scooted over to Mac's side of the bed. If she lay over there, she reasoned, she might not feel quite so dead inside.

It was there, nestled against the hard plaster wall, and curled into a fetal position, that Ella finally managed to cry herself to sleep.

The next morning, as Ella lifted her head off the pillow, and slowly opened her swollen and bleary eyes, a pounding so fierce it was nearly audible rumbled through her head. It was several moments before she realized that the pounding was coming from outside the building, and not inside her head.

Although, much to her dismay, her head was indeed throbbing with pain. Such a delightful combination, this inside and outside pounding, she thought dryly.

Luckily the baby was still sound asleep from his three a.m. feeding. Sitting up, she pushed back her hair and squinted into the bright sunlit room, a little glimmer of hope that Mac might just be there, in the back of her mind. But, alas, she saw as her gaze traveled around the room, he was nowhere to be found. Had she really expected anything else?

It was already late in the day. After eight o'clock. Ella

never slept this late, unless she was deathly sick. Pushing back the covers, she slowly stood and padded over to the cracked mirror that hung above the kitchen sink. Gasping, she took stock of what the night had wrought. She looked deathly sick, so she guessed that accounted for the late hour of the day.

Her eyes were red-rimmed and puffy, her complexion pale, her cheeks mottled. A tangled mess from having been slept on wet, her hair stuck out at crazy angles to her head. If she hadn't been so completely devastated by Mac's leaving her, she might have burst out laughing, for surely a derelict alien had taken over her body.

Little Garth caught sight of his mother as she moved past his cradle and, his face puckering, began to cry.

"I know, sweet pea," Ella said dully, as she lifted the baby into her arms and began to unbutton the top buttons of her nightgown. "Mama looks scary. But a nice shower will do her a world of good," she sighed, and settled into the rocker to feed her son.

Catching sight of Mac's traveling bag next to the rocker, Ella did battle with another flood of tears. She would not cry. She could not afford the luxury. She had to get on with her life as soon as humanly possible. For her son's sake, if nothing else.

Still, she stared at the bag, wondering what she should do with it. No doubt, it wouldn't be missed. Poking around inside with her free hand, she discovered a change of clothing, a pair of his shoes and—her fingers probed the familiar object—a slipper she'd been missing since the morning after their wedding. A lump welled in her throat.

Her fingers tested the fabric, remembering and wondering why he'd kept such a scruffy old thing. Well, he certainly wouldn't miss it anymore.

Mac had the means to replace life's inconsequentials.

Including people it seemed, she thought uncharitably. She was in a most uncharitable mood that morning.

Suddenly, as she sat there moping, Ella fancied that she smelled fresh coffee wafting up through the hallway and into her room.

Had Clyde come home? Her heart picked up speed. Yes! Clyde was back. She needed to talk to Clyde, to cry on his shoulder. To be assured that everything would be all right. Eventually.

She sniffed again. Yes, it was coffee all right. And pancakes. Ella's mouth watered, and her stomach rumbled in protest of its neglect. She had not eaten since…well, since yesterday morning. Suddenly she was starving. As soon as Garth had had his fill, Ella tucked him back into his cradle for a snooze, and selecting a few fresh pieces from her meager wardrobe, shuffled into the tiny bathroom for a quick shower. Improving her appearance might improve her outlook, she reasoned.

After she'd blow-dried her hair, and applied some makeup that she hoped concealed most of her crying jag, Ella changed and dressed Garth. Then, the two of them headed downstairs to the diner for the first time in the baby's life.

"This is the front door, where everyone always comes in," Ella whispered into her son's tiny ear, her running patter keeping her from dwelling on Mac.

Familiar sounds and smells greeted her as she opened the door to the dining room. The murmur of the regular clientele, the staticky radio playing a tragic country song and the hiss of the grill. Onions, stale tobacco and hickory smoked bacon. It was good to have Clyde back. At least some things remained the same in this unstable world.

All the usuals were there, from the look of things. Ella forced a wooden smile to her lips as she entered the room.

The cowbell jangling over the door had heads craning in their booths, to glimpse the newcomer.

As Ella moved through the busy diner, everyone called in greeting, and wanted a peek at the newest member of the skimpy population of Dogleg. As politely as possible, Ella obliged, anxious to get out of the limelight and back to Clyde.

"Why, hey there, Babe," Selma Jessop called. "Look, Barney, she's got her boy with her. Come here, honey, and give us a looky-see."

Ella shuffled forward and held Garth low for their inspection.

"Oh, Barn, will ya just look at those dimples?" Selma crowed gleefully.

"He's a looker, Babe," Barney conceded. "Ya did good."

"Thank you. He looks a lot like his father," Ella mused, still shrouded in her own pain-fogged world.

"I'll say he does," Selma chimed in, tugging on the receiving blanket and blowing kisses at the baby. "You here to work today, Babe?"

"I thought I might put together a pie or two, since I'm feeling so...fine," she lied and smiled brightly.

"Well, that's wonderful. She's gonna go back and bake a couple pies. How romantic. Ain't that romantic, Barney?"

"Mmm," Barney grunted affably.

Romantic? Ella must feel worse than she feared, for it seemed people were no longer making any sense.

"Give me that baby," Selma ordered and held out her meaty arms. Lifting him out of Ella's hands, the grandmotherly woman clutched the wriggling bundle to her massive bosom. "You go on in the kitchen for a while, honey.

I'll take care of this little sweet potato for you, while you go and get back in the swing of things.''

"Uh, okay, thank you," Ella murmured, grateful for the reprieve. It would be easier to cry on Clyde's shoulder without having to worry about Garth.

On her way into the kitchen, Ella nearly collided with a young girl wearing an apron and carrying several plates of food.

"Oh, uh, eh…excuse me," she stammered, staring after the girl as she headed out into the dining room.

"No problem," the girl called with a giggle. "This is my first day, so I'm a little clumsy."

First day? Ella wondered incredulously. Clyde had hired another helper? That didn't sound like Clyde. Her eyes traveled to the grill.

That didn't look like Clyde.

She blinked.

That wasn't Clyde.

That was Mac Brubaker. And he was a sight for sore— and red-rimmed—eyes.

Standing openmouthed, Ella stared at him as he slaved over the grill. The pancakes were lopsided and unequally loaded with blueberries, but they weren't burning, and they smelled good. Same with the bacon and eggs and hash browns. Well, the hash browns were a little on the dark hash brown side, she amended with a small smile, but nevertheless, they, too, looked edible. Nonplussed, Ella continued to stare in speechless wonder as he worked.

"What are you doing?" she finally managed to ask.

With a typical Brubaker deep-dimpled grin, he shrugged and flipped a pancake. "Cooking."

"Cooking," she repeated dully. "Where's Clyde?"

"Clyde?" Mac pretended to think a moment. "Oh, Clyde. The guy who used to own this place."

"*Used* to?"

"Mmm-hmm. He called about an hour ago from the Bahamas. He and the widow Perkins have tied the knot and are most likely working on their tans about now. Said for me to give you and the baby a kiss. I wasn't sure if he meant Garth or not, so I kissed the grill for good measure. Before I turned it on, of course," he amended good-naturedly. "I'm not *that* stupid."

An ebullient smile battled its way to the corners of Ella's lips. "Where did you learn how to cook?"

"Well, you'll have to ask the gang out front if I actually have learned to cook or not, but this much I watched Clyde do, the day I bought the diner from him. And last night I burned the midnight oil reading some old cookbooks and trying out some new recipes. Check out the garbage pail. My first pancakes were a little...tough." He grinned. "Gives me a whole new respect for Bertha, I'll tell you," he admitted with a chuckle.

"*You* bought the diner?"

"Mmm-hmm," came his nonchalant answer. "Didn't you see the sign out front? Papa Mac's Diner and Pie Shoppe. I was afraid I was going to wake you and the baby with all the racket I made nailing up the new part."

"You did."

"Sorry." His grin turned sheepish.

"*Papa* Mac's?"

"Yeah. Has a nice ring, don't you think?" Mac began turning the bacon with tongs. "Yep, Uncle Clyde and I—we struck a deal. He wanted to take his woman to Disney World, and I...well, I wanted to stay in Dogleg with mine."

"No," she whispered in disbelief.

"You should go look for yourself," Mac mumbled, busily conferring back and forth between the scrawled handwriting on the order sheets and the contents of his grill. "I painted it myself. Looks pretty good, if you're not too critical."

"Mac?"

"Hmm?"

"Really. The truth. What are you doing here?"

"Okay," he said and shrugged as he flipped and smashed and scraped and scrambled, "I figured, hey, if you don't feel that you can fit into my life, that's all right. Lord knows you have good reason, considering the ridiculous plans you overheard my family and their friends making."

"I do…"

"I'm sure that scene would have given even the most confident debutante a bad case of low self-esteem. But, if it makes you feel any better, I don't think they meant any of it the way it came across. They were just carried away with what they thought was a brilliant plan. I'm not surprised that you would take it personally. Anyone would."

"Anyone?"

Mac paused in his cooking efforts and looked deeply into her eyes. "Sure. *I* sure as heck would have. And I want you to know that I understand what you went through. And I don't blame you for anything."

Tears of joy sprang unbidden in her eyes. "You don't?"

"No. So, I figure if we're going to be together as a family, I'll just have to fit into your life." Looking around, he rolled his eyes. "And Clyde's. Took me all night just to figure out where everything is in this kitchen. Clyde was rather disorganized," he grumbled good-naturedly. "Had to hire Beth, right in the middle of her toast this morning, because I couldn't keep up. She was on her way to Dallas to look for work, so it was perfect. We're a little rough around the edges this morning, but, eventually, we'll settle into some sort of happy pattern." He beamed at her.

"No..." Still in shock, a dazed smile slowly spread across Ella's face as comprehension dawned. A happy tear trickled down her cheek. "You're *staying* in Dogleg?"

"Yep."

"For good?"

"If that's what we decide."

"What about Holly?"

"Holly?" A pained expression crossed his face. "What about her?" He waved a spatula in irritation. "It's a truly wacky tale, but you're going to have to believe me on this." His intense gaze tangled with her liquid one, begging her to understand and believe. "I was never really engaged to her. Honestly." Sending his spatula over his shoulder and clattering onto the counter, he moved to stand directly in front of her, and took her hands in his. "It was all just a ruse to keep Big Daddy off my back about getting married. Since Holly's parents were driving her crazy about settling down, she was thrilled with the idea of a pretend engagement. I barely saw her all summer. We thought of it as a big practical joke. Too bad the joke ended up being on us. But at least it bought me the precious time I needed to look for you."

"The engagement was never real? Truly?" she breathed, barely daring to believe.

"Yes. Truly. Cross my heart." He brought her delicate fingers to his chest and drew a cross over his heart. "It's a long, rather sad story, but suffice it to say that Holly is no more interested in marrying me, than I am in her. She knows all about you, by the way."

"She does?" Ella's expression was incredulous.

Mac nodded, and thoughtfully stroked the sandy stubble that graced his jaw. "You'll really like her. I'm pretty sure she'll still be at the ranch when we return to tell everyone we're married, because, if I'm not mistaken, she's busy falling in love with my little brother at the moment.''

Ella stared at him, barely daring to believe. ''B...b...but what about our divorce?''

''What divorce? I never signed the papers you sent. Did you run off to some foreign country and get a divorce?''

Ella shook her head. ''No,'' she whispered.

''Then I guess we've been married for nearly a year now.''

''We have?''

''Pretty close.'' Cupping her chin in his hand, he tilted her face up to his. ''Happy anniversary, a little bit early,'' he whispered, then placed a tender kiss, as light as a hummingbird's wings, on her slackened lips.

When he pulled away Ella stared at the man who would do all this for her, with tears glistening. Suddenly she was able to see her worth through his eyes, and she was incredibly touched. Never in her entire life had anybody ever been willing to go to such lengths for her.

He must love her more than words could possibly describe, if he was willing to give up his life of luxury and high finance and stay here in Dogleg as the owner of this dismal diner. Would this man never cease to amaze her? To make her love him?

He was just like a prince in a fairy tale.

And she, his princess.

''Mac,'' she whispered, her throat closing with emotion, ''this is all too much.''

Sighing, Mac allowed his forehead to drop against hers. ''What will it take to make you understand that you are not getting rid of me? Ever?''

''But...I...I can't ask you to leave your life.''

''No,'' he murmured, gathering her into his arms, oblivious to the smoke that belched from his now burning grill, "you can't ask me to leave my wife."

And with that, his mouth claimed hers for a kiss that would seal their love for time and eternity.

Senora Baxter, in her position as the one paying entt,
had elected to be exactly her wife.
"And you said Mr. Diaz claimed he'd stolen the ph
wouldn't leave their trap for three days," Kelly.

Chapter Eleven

"Are you sure you want to move back to the ranch?"
Mac asked Ella as they loaded their meager belongings into
some cardboard boxes that he'd unearthed from the kitchen.
"It's not too late to change your mind. Clyde is still willing
to have us stay on as partners."

Ella shook her head slowly, already a little homesick,
but knowing that this time she was making the right decision to leave. "Clyde and his new wife will get along just
fine without us. Especially with Beth's help."

"Just checking." Mac nodded, satisfied with her answer.

Over a week had passed, since Clyde and his new bride
had returned from their honeymoon, glowing with newly
wedded bliss. Even so, Ella could tell by the way the old
man had hung around the diner—even after he'd showed
them the dozens of pictures he'd taken of Disney World—
that he was looking for something to do with his days.

So before either man knew what had hit them, they'd
struck up another bargain. Partners. They would co-own the

best little diner this side of the Mississippi. There was even some talk of expansion down the line. Franchises.

And, though Mac had appeared delighted with the new partnership, claiming it would give him more time with his wife and son, Ella knew better. Though he would never admit it, he was longing for his executive seat back at Brubaker International. And, for the love and laughter that his own boisterous family provided.

"You know," Mac said as he paused to pick up Garth who lay fussing in his cradle, "we don't have to move back to the ranch. We could go anywhere you want. The sky is the limit." Expertly he patted the baby's back, rocking back and forth, soothing the fussy cry.

"No, Mac. It's time that I stopped running. I want to go back to your family. I—" she stopped folding the baby's clothes and faced him, with a longing to finally set down some roots stinging the back of her throat "—want to meet you halfway. You taught me that, Mac. I've lived my life long enough without a family. How could I, in good conscience, deprive our baby of doting grandparents, and a host of loving aunts and uncles?"

A small smile of understanding tipped the corner of his lips. "He'll certainly have that."

"I know," she whispered, loving the picture her two men made, sandy heads together, dimples in full bloom. Ella wanted her son to have everything that she'd never had as a child: a big, loving family.

She also wanted more for her husband, than to give up his life and career with Brubaker International in order to run a greasy spoon. Eventually the challenge would grow old for an adventurous man like Mac. The fact that he bought the diner was a touching gesture, but Ella was ready to go home.

Home to the Brubakers. Home to her new family.

"Well," Ella sighed, and looked around at the now-empty room that had been her home for the better part of a year, "I guess once we get these last few boxes down to the Jeep, we'll be ready to go." She smoothed her crisp traveling suit over her newly slender figure, still having a hard time getting used to the fashionable wardrobe that Mac had insisted she needed. It was true. Her paltry collection of clothing had been a disgrace. Giving her upswept bun a pat into place, she nodded.

"Okay. I'll take the boxes, if you want to take the baby and go say your goodbyes to Clyde."

Pinching her lips between her fingers to stem a tide of emotion, Ella smiled a watery smile at Mac. Once again, she was finding herself leaving a person, and a town she'd grown to love. "Okay," she murmured haltingly and, taking a step forward, lifted the baby from Mac's arms. "I'll be along in a moment."

"Take your time." His eyes were gentle with compassion as he kissed the side of her head.

As Ella made her way downstairs to kiss Clyde's leathery cheek and make him promise to keep in touch, myriad worries plagued her mind. However, as Garth cooed and smiled a toothless smile up at her, she decided she was doing the right thing. For Mac. For the baby. For the Brubaker family.

But, most of all, for herself.

Later that day, when Ella and Mac arrived back at the ranch, it was obvious by the number of cars parked in the parking area that something big was going on out in the south courtyard. Country music flowed out to greet them, accompanied by the sound of rowdy voices and hoots of laughter. All this noise was underscored by Big Daddy's voice booming over a public address system.

Ella looked quizzically at Mac. "Perhaps this is not the perfect time to announce that you are married and have a son?"

Mac appreciated the glint of amusement in her eye. "Perhaps not," came his droll response. "Why don't you go shock the loafers off Bertha and the gang in the kitchen, and I'll meet you in there, once I've discovered what's going on out here. We can decide when to make our announcement, once we get the lay of the land."

"Excellent idea," Ella agreed. "Come on, Garth," she prattled, "let's go say hi to Auntie Bertha."

Ella could tell by the grudging smile that forced its way into Bertha's doughy cheeks, when she'd walked through the door for the first time in nearly a year, that the older woman had missed her more than she'd ever admit. That alone made the trip back worthwhile, in Ella's opinion. The months melted away, and suddenly, Ella felt as if she'd never left the Brubaker household. As if she'd never lived anywhere else. The feeling of homecoming was blissful.

Bertha was holding the baby against her round shoulder, patting him on the back and chatting ninety miles a minute with Ella, when Mac finally made it back into the kitchen.

"Yes, ma'am," Bertha crowed, "old Stormy's back from her coma. Delilah Chastain lost her memory, and now—get this—she's a pussycat! Nice as pie, and the mayor, that handsome Rafe Donovan, wants to marry her, can you believe that?"

Ella smiled. Good for Stormy. Now she could live her life with a clear conscience knowing that Stormy and the girls were, at the very least, able to eat.

Stumbling up behind them, Mac leaned heavily against the countertop. "Got an extra steak you're not using?" he muttered, and strode to the refrigerator as if not a moment had passed since he'd last breezed through the door.

"Lord have mercy, boy," Bertha shouted, staring agog at Mac, "what the devil happened to your eye?"

"And," Ella gasped, taking in the contusions, abrasions and lacerations on her poor husband's face, "Your... your...mouth...and your...jaw?" Leaping off her chair, she rushed to the freezer and helped him load a plastic bag with ice cubes.

"Well," Mac said with a lopsided grin, once Ella began ministering to his multitude of wounds, "it would seem that I have good news."

"*Good* news?" Ella stared at him. "What's that?" she wondered dubiously as she rinsed a clean cloth out under the faucet and began to stem the different trickles of blood.

"My little brother and Holly are getting married. They just announced it, down at Holly's bridal shower. And I gotta say that they're perfect for each other. They both pack a mean wallop."

"*What?*" Bertha groused and shifted little Garth to her other shoulder as if he were a ten-pound bag of spuds. "I'm just getting used to the idea that she ain't marrying you, boy! Now she's marrying *Buck?* What the devil is going on in this family?"

"Yep." His grin became more of a grimace as Ella, having opened the kitchen's first-aid kit, found the hydrogen peroxide and began to apply it to the deeper cuts. "And they couldn't be happier."

"If they're so happy," Ella asked with a puzzled frown, "then what happened to your face?"

"This?" Mac gestured loosely to his head. "Oh, this is just Buck's way of telling me his good news."

Ella giggled. "I take it that Holly was not happy to be left holding the bag?"

"Uh-huh."

"And I suppose Buck was not too happy to discover that Holly was never really engaged to you all summer?"

"Ahhh...no." Mac hung his head, looking contrite.

"So," Ella said as she continued dabbing with her cotton swab, "he probably felt a little duped and maybe—" she paused in her ministrations and pretended to think "—a little like he wasted a lot of valuable time that could have been spent with the woman he loves?"

"Very perceptive."

"I know how he feels," Ella sighed.

"Sorry." Mac boyishly looked up at her through his good eye.

Bertha snorted. "Serves ya right for lying to us all and putting us all through hell for the last year or so." Grumbling and shaking her head, Bertha acted as if she'd been personally affronted by the hijinks of her boys.

"You're right, Bertha," Mac agreed. "I deserve this." He lightly touched the bulge above his eye. "And more. I suppose Big Daddy and Miss Clarise will be only too happy to give me an earful, once they get their hands on me." He squinted morosely up at Ella. "I don't even want to think what the Fergusons will have to say."

Looping her arms around his shoulders, Ella gently placed her cheek against the one spot that hadn't been beaten to a pulp by his younger brother. "Don't worry, sweetheart," she said. "You'll always have me."

"I know." Mac's reply was hoarse as he kissed her hand.

Bertha nuzzled Garth's smooth cheek. "Land o' Goshen, the world had surely turned upside down today." Pretending to huff, she buried her red face into the baby's neck and whispered, "But I'm glad."

After Mac and Ella had bid the kitchen staff a good-night, and gathered little Garth from Bertha's firm grasp, they'd headed up to Mac's old suite. So far, only the kitchen staff knew that Mac was not alone.

Once inside the fabulous suite, Ella could see that Mac had already had their boxes of personal effects delivered. Her gaze traveled over the beautiful room, admiring its rich, romantic decor. Wandering over to the fireplace, Ella ran a hand lightly across the marble surface.

"So," she murmured in awe, "this is where you grew up."

"Like it?"

"No."

"No?" A troubled frown graced his brow.

"I *love* it," she breathed, and turned toward him, her face radiant.

"Good," Mac sighed in relief and, laying the baby down on the bed, crossed the room and swept her into his arms. "Welcome home, Mrs. Brubaker."

Through the open windows, the last remnants of the roaringly successful bridal shower for Holly filtered into the room along with the late summer breezes.

"Thank you, Mr. Brubaker. It feels good to be home." And now, she thought as her husband gingerly claimed her mouth for a long tender kiss, she understood what Mac meant when he'd proposed. With him by her side, she could conquer the world.

It was the dead of night when the phone rang at the Brubaker residence. Groggily Big Daddy fumbled for the alarm clock and when it wouldn't shut off, tried the phone.

"Yep?" he barked, still thrashing around in the pitch-dark, looking for the knob to the lamp. Blinding light finally filled the room, sending Big Daddy reeling back on the bed, his arm thrown over his eyes.

"Wha...wha...what?" he finally grunted, getting the mouthpiece to the instrument sorted out and aimed at his mouth. "Yeah? What? Yeah? What? Yeah? What? *What! Yeah! Oh, yeah!* I'll tell her! We'll be there. Visiting hours? Eight to ten in the morning. We'll do it. Okay, boy. We sure love you. Congratulations."

Too excited to find the cradle, Big Daddy hung up the phone on the alarm clock and didn't seem to notice that the electronic operator repeatedly encouraged him to "Please, hang up, and try his call again."

"Lamb chop," Big Daddy crowed at Miss Clarise who was now sitting straight up in bed and looking with rabid curiosity at her husband as he flailed his way out of bed. "That was Bru! Penelope had the baby! We're grandparents!" he shouted.

"How wonderful!" Miss Clarise cried. "Grandparents!"

"Yessiree! Two grandparents."

"Of course." Miss Clarise waved an impatient hand. "What did they have?"

"Two!" Big Daddy rumbled.

"*Two?* Twins?" Thunderstruck, Miss Clarise simply stared.

"Yup! Both girls!"

"Girls!" she breathed ecstatically.

"Named 'em Wynonna and Naomi."

"How lovely."

"I think so," Big Daddy roared, fishing a cigar out of his pocket and lighting it up. "Both the girls and Mama are fine. I'm gonna go tell the kids!" Overjoyed and bursting with enthusiasm, Big Daddy charged into the hallway, leaving a jet stream of cigar smoke in his wake.

Running down the upstairs hallway, the new grandpa began beating on doors. "Bru called! The baby is here! I mean, the babies are here!'' he called breathlessly, reminiscent of Paul Revere on another historical night.

Buck poked his head out of his room, half awake, but his dimples in full bloom. Across the hall, Holly peeked out of her door and caught his heavy-lidded gaze. ''The baby is here?''

They smiled for a long, loving moment at each other, each thinking of the day when it would be their turn.

''That is wonderful,'' they agreed.

Meanwhile Big Daddy was still pounding on doors and after waking most of the family finally arrived at Mac's door.

''Mac! Wake up! The baby is here!'' Big Daddy roared, nearly knocking the doors off their hinges in his enthusiasm.

The noise must have reminded Garth that it was near his feeding time, as his earsplitting cries could be heard out into the hallway.

Big Daddy frowned.

As Mac opened the door to his suite, his squalling baby bobbing haplessly in the crook of his arm, he grinned broadly at his father. ''Yes, Big Daddy, you're right about that. The baby is here. Big Daddy, I'd like you to meet your grandson, Garth.''

Big Daddy took one look at little Garth and, his eyes rolling back in his head, fainted dead away.

''Perhaps,'' Mac said drolly to Ella as she rushed to Big Daddy's side, ''this was not the perfect time to tell him our news.''

Chapter Twelve

In the wee hours of that night—after Big Daddy had regained consciousness—the entire family gathered downstairs around the enormous kitchen table. Johnny, Kenny, Waylon, Willie and little Hank all tousle-haired and grinning sleepily, shuffled into the kitchen. Sniffing inquisitively at the tantalizing aroma that wafted from the oven, they all found seats to flop into around one end of the table. Patsy, who was still studying dance in Europe, had been told the happy news by phone. At the other end of the table, Holly and Buck sat across from Mac. Ella was busy with Miss Clarise, pulling cobblers out of the oven, and loading bowls for the hungry crowd.

At the head of the table, Big Daddy held Garth on his knee, bobbing and bouncing the little guy till Miss Clarise finally cried whiplash, and forced him to slap a bridle on his enthusiasm.

"I'm sorry, lovedoodle, but you have to admit, it's not every day that a man becomes a grandfather." Clasping his firstborn grandson lovingly to his chest, his weathered face beamed as he roared, *"Three times over!"*

As if he understood what was being said, little Garth waved his tiny fists and crowed.

Over bowls full of Ella's piping hot peach cobbler topped with vanilla ice cream, Mac pulled Ella into the chair at his side and finally began to regale everyone with his own tale of marriage and parenthood. Amid much gasping, chastisement and laughter on the part of his family, the details of his elopement and less than serious engagement to Holly came forth.

Holy's cheeks flared bright red as everyone stared at her, mouths slack.

"You were only *pretendin'* to be engaged?" Big Daddy gasped, his elastic brows arched high with wonder. "But why?"

"It seemed like a good idea, at the time," Holly lamely explained and shrugged. "I'm really sorry. Please, uh…" She cleared her throat and looked at her future in-laws with a plea for mercy in her sorrowful gaze. "Forgive me."

Ella smiled at her and patted her hand.

"And me, too," Mac chimed in. "It was my idea as much as it was hers. I take the lion's share of the blame."

"Well." Big Daddy harrumphed, feeling far too jovial to split hairs. "I guess I should apologize, too. I kinda forced your hand by pushin' you two together that way. None of this mess would have happened if I hadn't interfered. I'm—" his face bunched into a leathery wad of remorse "—sorry."

Miss Clarise sighed, but remained silent, a small smile tipping the corners of her mouth.

"Then again," Big Daddy explained, pressing his lopsided grin to the top of Garth's head, "if I hadn't interfered,

I might not have ended up with this precious bundle of joy.''

Everyone groaned. Miss Clarise rolled her eyes.

''You almost didn't end up with him anyway,'' Mac said, picking up the threads of his story with Ella, and explaining how he'd arrived in the middle of the night to deliver the baby. ''To be perfectly honest, with no doctor or phone, we were both pretty scared for a while there.''

Then came the question Ella was dreading most.

''Honey pie, why did you run off in the first place?'' Big Daddy asked gently, and peered into her large, liquid eyes.

''Well...'' Not knowing what to say, she glanced up at Mac for guidance. He nodded for her to tell the whole story, so, taking a deep breath, Ella plunged in. ''It was, um, something that I...well, I...overheard in the library.''

Slowly Miss Clarise began to nod, a look of sympathy on her sweet face. ''The day the Fergusons came to visit?''

''Yes,'' Ella murmured.

''Ahh. I'm not surprised.''

''What?'' Big Daddy looked back and forth between his wife and daughter-in-law.

''It was the morning after Mac and I eloped.''

The memories began to churn in the old man's head, and his face crumpled in shame. ''Uh-oh.''

''Oh, you poor darlin','' Miss Clarise murmured, reaching next to her and clasping Ella's hand. ''How you must have suffered.''

Swallowing, Ella blinked and nodded. ''A little,'' she admitted. ''I knew I would never fit in...so I left, deciding it would be in everyone's best interest.''

''Never fit it?'' Big Daddy shouted in disbelief. ''Why, darlin', this place hasn't been the same without you at all.''

''It's true,'' Miss Clarise told her. ''Big Daddy was beside himself when you left. In a very short time, you became like a daughter to us. Especially with our Patsy being in Europe. That's why he didn't like the idea of Mac chasing you off with his flirtatious ways. Big Daddy wanted you to stay. Not go.''

"But as a member of the staff."

Big Daddy vehemently shook his head. "No! Member of the staff, member of the family, member of the hair club for men! I don't care, honeydew. I just didn't want you to leave. Heck, sugar, I picked ya out of that truck stop because I knew there was somethin' special about you. And when you up and left, we all missed you somethin' fierce. Even Bertha, and she don't miss nobody. Why, we all considered you family from the moment you arrived. And now that you're one of my three precious daughters-in-law, why I couldn't be happier.''

Tears of joy were streaming down Ella's cheeks. "Thank you," she murmured. "That means more to me than you'll ever know.''

Mac looped an arm around her shoulders, pulled her into the warm curve of his body and planted a loving kiss at the top of her head. Eyes shining, she looked up at him. For the first time in her life, Ella Brubaker had everything she'd ever dreamed of as a little girl. And more. Her dreams had come true, and she was beginning to live happily ever after.

"I'm so sorry that you misunderstood me and Miss Clarise and the Fergusons talking in the library," Big Daddy said. "We were understandably excited about the idea of a family bond with our good friends. But—" he shrugged happily "—thanks to Buck, that's all been taken care of.''

Big Daddy winked at Holly.

"You know, I've been told by more than one person to stop interfering in my kids' lives, but I just can't seem to help myself! But that's okay. I'm just glad that we're all back together now.'' He looked around the table, his eyes dewy with emotion. ''And lucky me! I have three of the finest daughters-in-law I could ever dream of! And three beautiful new grandbabies! All named for—'' his throat closed off with emotion for a moment ''—my favorite country singers. How could I be so lucky?''

''I don't know, Big Daddy, but you do seem to land on your feet every time.'' Mac chuckled. His gaze traveled down the table to his unmarried siblings. ''All I can say to the rest of you is look out, because I doubt he's learned his lesson.''

The boys at the end of the table groaned and shook their heads at each other, for soon they would be approaching marriageable age.

Slapping his knee, Big Daddy howled with laughter at their bleak expressions. ''You got that right, son! You got that right.''

* * * * *

Don't you fret. Big Daddy's still got plenty of children to marry off. This time, it's his daughter Patsy who's about to take the marriage plunge. Look for her story as THE BRUBAKER BRIDES *series continues in December from Silhouette Romance!*

MATERNITY LEAVE

Coming September 1998

Three delightful stories about the blessings
and surprises of "Labor" Day.

TABLOID BABY by Candace Camp

She was whisked to the hospital in the nick of time....

THE NINE-MONTH KNIGHT
by Cait London

A down-on-her-luck secretary is experiencing
odd little midnight cravings....

THE PATERNITY TEST by Sherryl Woods

The stick turned blue before her
biological clock struck twelve....

*These three special women are very pregnant...and very
single, although they won't be either for too much longer,
because baby—and Daddy—are on their way!*

Available at your favorite retail outlet.

Look us up on-line at: http://www.romance.net   PSMATLEV